Capture

Diamondsong

A Concerto in Ten Parts

Part 02:
Capture

E.D.E. Bell

Atthis Arts
Detroit, Michigan

Diamondsong
Part 02: Capture

This is a work of fiction.
Any resemblance to actual pyrsi, winged or otherwise, is purely coincidental.

Cover Art by M.C. Krauss

Map of Ada-ji by Ulla Thynell

Interior Design by G.C. Bell

Editorial Services by:
Camille Gooderham Campbell
Catherine Jones Payne and Haley Tomaszewski, Quill Pen Editorial
M. Cusack

Published by Atthis Arts, LLC
Detroit, Michigan
atthisarts.com

ISBN 978-1-945009-28-0

Library of Congress Control Number: 2018911339

First Edition: Published October 2018

This book is dedicated to Meghan Cusack.

Forever grateful for your insights and generosity.

Preface

You turned the page!

Ok, so if you are still as traumatized by Grover's classic story as I am, you'll know that means I'm waggling my hands that you're here. That you've probably read *Escape*, and you're interested in continuing Dime's story. Except in this case, Grover's discouragement is a metaphor for my own inner fears. But now we're here together, on the next page.

That makes me really happy.

In fact, I'm not going to say much more than that. Thank you for being here with me and thank you for wanting to know what happens next.

I would, of course, like to express my gratitude to the pyrsi who made this possible. Thanks to another great editorial review by Catherine and Haley at Quill Pen Editorial. I'm so glad Catherine pushed me on a few key things; the story is much better for it. And my heartfelt thanks to the team: Camille Gooderham Campbell, Meghan Cusack, Sasha Kasoff Moore, Deborah Reilly, Laura Johnson, and Trowby Brockman.

Talk more next time? For now, let's get to it. We have a fairy leader to find.

Cheers,

E.D.E. Bell
October 2018

The World of Ada-ji

The Ja-lal: A humanoid species, dwelling in the foothills and plains of Ada-ji, characterized by broad advancements in construction, invention, and health. The Fo-ror call them brutes.

The Fo-ror: A winged humanoid species, dwelling in the forests of Ada-ji, characterized by their natural living and the use of magical powers, known as valence. The Ja-lal call them fairies.

The Ja-lal and Fo-ror are similar in form, with gray skin, but differences between them in composition and culture. Pyr is singular for a Ja-lal or Fo-ror and pyrsi is plural.

The pyrsi of Ada-ji hold many **gender identities**. While this doesn't clarify all aspects of gender, it is polite to introduce oneself with a prefix, indicating the appropriate pronouns:

Fe' indicates a set of feminine identities, using the pronouns she/her/her(s).

Ma' indicates a set of masculine identities, using the pronouns he/him/his.

Ji' indicates a set of spectrum identities, using the pronouns ve/ver/vis.

When gender is unknown, it is polite to refer to a pyr with xe/xem/xyr(s). Any group of pyrsi (plural) would be referred to with they/them/their(s).

A pyr may be generically referred to as **Burge**, short for the more formal Burgess, often for purposes of polite address or getting a stranger's attention. This is similar to the use of Sir or Ma'am on Earth. For those who hold social prejudice based on class, the term implies some sense of status or honor.

Ja-lal and Fo-ror may live up to 50 cycles. Their lives are divided into defined **epochs**, aligning with societal expectations:

Aoch Age 0-9 — Characterized by upbringing, education, and exploration

Bakh Age 10-19 — Centered on building family, performing and completing apprenticeships, and finalizing life plans

Gamh Age 20-29 — Fully immersed in their specialty or role, contributing full-time to society

Dorh Age 30-39 — Respected in leadership and/or advisory roles; it is normal to take some time for self

Eroh Age 40+ — Expected to retire and engage in craft or occasional consulting, through the **life expectancy of around 50 cycles**.

Expectations differ for each culture. For example, while a Ja-lal must develop xyr profession into a career, a Fo-ror's profession and rank are set based on xyr social class and other historical and cultural factors.

A **cycle** on Ada-ji is perhaps up to four times the length of an Earth year. So, our main character, at age 20.5 cycles, has lived more than 80 Earth years but, in relation to her life span, could be considered at the **maturity of her early forties** on Earth.

Each **turn** on Ada-ji, a period of day and then night, is **significantly longer than an Earth day**. As such, pyrsi do not sleep according to light or dark, but instead based on their own needs, lifestyle, profession, and schedule.

The Ja-lal measure time by the periodic sounding of bells; they refer to the resultant time periods with the same term. The Fo-ror are less rigid about time-keeping and refer to the equivalent time period as a span. Each **bell**, or **span**, consists of more than two Earth hours.

Smaller amounts of time are referred to by both cultures as **takes**, which can be thought of as about ten Earth minutes.

In Earth terms, it has been about three weeks since the beginning of our tale.

The Ja-lal and Fo-ror live on separate sides of the Great Cliff. They have not interacted since the *Great War*, an event most noted for being the **end of the Violence** on Ada-ji.

SYNOPSIS TO HERE

Fe'Diamond, known as Dime, had just left her career working for the Circles, the government of the Ja-lal. Suddenly, three hooded figures burst into her home with ropes, demanding to take her away. Without any understanding of why this had occurred, Dime and her spouse, Dayn, ran to escape them.

The intruders were revealed to be Fo-ror, commonly known as fairies. These fairies, unseen since the conclusion of the Great War, were feared and loathed by the Ja-lal, who were taught that any contact would cause the Violence to return. The fairies were said to employ a magical power known as valence, but Dime had thought this a myth—perhaps that even the fairies themselves were a myth—until she saw both herself.

Trying to protect pyrsi from the fairies, she escaped from the city, now separated from Dayn and with the fairies in continued pursuit. In an attempt to finally evade them, she ended up falling over the Great Cliff, landing in the forest and lying unconscious for a spell. She was carried away to a beach by a large animal known as a newt, where she stayed among their troop as she recovered. There, she befriended the young one who had found her, whom she called Juni. It became apparent to her that the Fo-ror had driven the newts from their original home, keeping them away from Fo-ror civilization—and consequently from fresh water—with large barriers of rope netting.

A fellow Ja-lal, named Ella, found Dime with the newts and helped her return to her homeland, Sol's Reach. Ella told Dime that her late spouse had been a Fo-ror, and so she had a special interest in any interactions between the two species.

They headed for Dime's home in the large Ja-lal city of Lodon, but found it stirred up by a fringe political group named Sol's Pillars.

Ella insisted it would be unwise to enter the city, and instead she took Dime to her own home, on the edge of the old woods. Here, Ella reluctantly explained that Dime was, biologically, a Fo-ror—one whose wings had been removed as an infant. They also surmised that the invaders had been representatives of the Seats, the Fo-ror government.

Frustrated by the lack of information, Dime resolved to travel to the forest city of Pito, in Fo-ror lands, to ask the Seats directly what all of this was about. Ella was at first shocked, but she agreed to help so long as Dime stayed at her house a while to heal and restock her supplies before leaving. Dime agreed.

Ada-Ji
N
S
E
W

Capture

Do you see a person skilled in their work?
They will stand before Kings;
they will not stand before obscure people.

—Proverbs 22:29, *The Sayings of the Wise,*
c950 BCE, as adapted by a friend, 2017

Act 1

Terms

"You still doing this?" Ella asked. Behind her, the kettle started to steam.

"Delightfully rhetorical," Dime murmured, running her fingers through Friend's plump needles. Ella seemed increasingly concerned about Dime's decision to travel to Pito, but Dime was going, and she wasn't changing her mind.

This was also something she needed to do alone. Instinct told her that. Ella had offered to go with her, but Dime had reasoned it would help her more if Ella stayed back, keeping an eye on events in the city, and on Dime's family. And if anything went wrong in Pito, someone would know where Dime had gone. Ella had finally agreed.

"I'll take another cup, if you don't mind," she added, lifting her hand from Ella's evergreen companion to motion toward the stove.

As Ella poured the hot water over the brew beans, a nutty aroma filled the tower room. Dime breathed in deep, then returned to packing her things. She folded a pair of thick socks and pushed them into an inside pocket of her new backpack.

Ella was quite the tailor. Dime now had a full ensemble, with at least one extra of everything. As her usual velour had already proven not great for travel, this new set was mostly a plain, sturdy fabric, yet still dark in color. She'd have to do without the usual glass and metal accents she liked; she wanted to minimize anything that could draw attention.

Perhaps not wanting her to be *too* plain, Ella had worked in a few embroidered vines along the garments' edges, echoing Dime's facial tattoos. On top of that, her new jacket had about every clip and pocket Dime could ever want, and the arms actually fit right. With her petite height and plump build, her arms *never* fit quite right.

Dime's wardrobe was accompanied by an expertly-made pair of boots, oiled on the outside—Ella said this was for keeping out water—and cushy on the inside. She also had something called tree shoes, which Ella indicated were for use on floors above ground level. Despite her nerves at how she'd be treated there, Dime was most curious to see what a fairy tower looked like.

She was less thrilled to carry a set of small flares Ella had given her. They were similar to the emergency flares travelers carried, but Ella said she'd ground and wrapped these herself and they had a unique color to them. Apparently, she gave them to a few contacts in the city in case they needed to reach her. Dime had started to ask if they could really be seen so far away, but when Ella started to brag about their "extra snap," Dime had decided she didn't need to know.

Less alarming, Ella had even given her a complete set of wood-handled tools, travel dishes, and miscellanea that must have taken a hearty dent from her savings—in addition to a full set of climbing gear from the storage room. Ella had completely eschewed the concept of repayment, insisting the existing debt of a good draught of ferm covered it. "I don't need it," she'd add, before changing the subject.

"I think that's everything," Dime said, leaning the large back-pack against the wall.

She sat back at the table, tilting her nose over the brew and enjoying the fragrant steam against her face. She was most definitely going to borrow one of those filter bags and take as many of the beans as she could reasonably carry. Her gaze wandered around the living floor, lined with small windows and colorful sketches of flowers and plants, each in a styled wood frame.

Even after only two turns here, Dime was going to miss this little tower. Nestled into the old woods with just four floors, it was spacious enough for living, but cozy compared to the massive towers of Lodon.

The ground floor held mostly storage, along with walkways to a pantry and a washroom. The second floor, where they sat now, held the cooking and living areas. Above was Ella's sleeping area, large enough to split with a guest. And above that was a small library, divided into three parts. Dime would have liked to have spent more time in the top rooms, but she sensed that Ella was protective of them and so she didn't push.

There was no more reason to delay, as Dime was feeling just about herself again. Her ankle was back to normal, and even the worst of her cuts had closed, replaced by angry little red lines to which she kept a layer of balm applied.

While Dime had rested, Ella had gone off to the city. When she'd returned, she reassured Dime that her family was well—her spouse, children, and father—and that she'd been able to deliver Dime's note to Dayn. Whom she noted to be charming, which made Dime smile.

Ella confessed that, from the little she'd seen, the situation had only worsened in the city. No more fairies had been spotted in Lodon, but Sol's Pillars had ensured the tension stayed high, keeping the incident fresh in everyone's minds. The Circles had barely maintained an overall state of calm, and Ella was worried what might happen if that balance tipped. One of the downfalls of a system predicated on obedience was the lack of safety net if that order fell.

Dime couldn't solve any of it herself; she wouldn't know where to start without more information. It was Intel she needed: knowledge, understanding, insight. So, today, she would go to Pito and learn what she could. Dime wasn't the best with big decisions; sometimes she just had to make them.

"Here," Ella said, holding out a dark, hooded cloak. By now, Dime knew to stifle her gut reaction against cloaks and hoods, which were strictly forbidden in the Ja-lal city of Lodon, where covering one's head spoke only of ill-intent. Besides, she didn't really want another lecture from Ella on the Circles' hypocrisy.

Not to say Ella was wrong. Dime was learning the hard way that the clean lines the Circles ensured everyone was taught weren't truly so clean. Hoods were forbidden to prevent pyrsi from hiding any hemsa, which denoted that a pyr had been convicted of a crime. It was a protection for all.

Yet these rules—they didn't just expose your hemsa; they exposed you. Everyone in plain sight of the Circles. A lack of public privacy for those who desired it. Also—and Dime had always said this—permanently marking pyrsi for all past crimes felt like something pyrsi should be protected *from*.

The same with the Violence. The Violence did not exist. It had been eradicated through the Ja-lal victory in the Great War. Ungranted touching, stealing, harm to property, these were no longer threats to the Ja-lal.

Then, if the Violence did not exist, what were the hemsa even for? For matters of distaste? It didn't make sense, once she'd considered it.

And the fairies, no one had seen them. But, Dime had seen them. Others had seen them. They weren't legendary; they lived right over the cliff. One could just *go* there.

All Dime's lines had started to blur, and what upset her the most was that it had taken a series of jarring events to blur them. Dime had always prided herself on reflection and thought.

She hadn't thought enough.

Doing her best to keep a calm face, Dime folded the cloak into the bag, pulling the embedded strings tight.

"If you wear it over the backpack, it might look as though you have wings," Ella said. "From a distance," she clarified.

Speaking of keeping fairies at a distance, there was a question she'd been meaning to ask. "The Light didn't give you a hemsa to keep you out of the city." Ella had told her that a previous Light, not Sala, had visited her and her Fo-ror spouse, Suzanne, ordering Suzanne to leave. When Suzanne refused—and no pyr refused the Light—he spread a story painting Ella as a hexing witch of legend, hoping at least to keep pyrsi from learning her secret.

Yet, a hemsa would have resolved the issue.

"Oh, no, hemsa aren't for secrets." Ella said with a squint. "Have you met anyone with a hemsa?" She waved off Dime's response. "No, not met them. *Known* them."

With the clarification added, Dime could only think of one pyr, and his hemsa was old and minor; friends had learned to overlook it. Not thinking that was Ella's intent, she shook her head.

"They can get a little reckless. Wouldn't you? If you can't fully return to society, if you're always an outcast, one starts to consider what's left to lose. They wanted to leave me with something to fear, not nothing to lose.

"Besides," Ella added a chuckle, "Suzanne wouldn't have let them. The way she told the Light to skedaddle back to his golden tower, he wasn't going to try a thing. The Light's power consists solely of that which pyrsi grant xem. Remember that."

Ella was always telling Dime to remember things, so she smiled politely. More interestingly, Dime had never heard of a hemsa being refused, whether directly or not.

Lines. So many lines.

Pyrsi like Ella and Suzanne threatened every method by which the Circles held order. They were *dangerous*. By dissent, not crime. By simply living outside the Circles' strict boundaries, they might show that those boundaries were subjective in the first place. Dime could imagine the Light's dilemma in hoping—gambling, really— that they would just stay away.

"The thing about hemsa," Ella continued, as she wiped off the table, "is they aren't offered the same to all. Who from the Circles have you met with hemsa-bearing family? Who from the upper class? Oh, but that's because the high class know how to behave. They are raised *properly*."

Dime cringed. Certainly upbringing impacted behavior, but when pre-judged by class, it sounded like a Sol's Pillars speech. She knew Ella was speaking satirically, but her words were uncomfortable to hear. "We'll see what the Seats think of my upbringing," she quipped, mostly out of unease.

Ella stopped in place, the dishcloth in her hand. Her lips tightened, and if she was going to say something, she didn't. But now she had Dime thinking. What would the Seats do? What would Dime do?

"I wish I knew what problem I was trying to solve." The words fell from her mouth, as if she'd been holding them there a while. "I'm going to Pito to find out why the Fo-ror wanted me—and why now." She left out *and why someone cut off my wings as an infant*, a crime whose magnitude had only been growing in her mind. "But if Sol's Pillars are rallying in Lodon, maybe the problem is in Lodon. Maybe this isn't just about me."

"Heh," Ella grunted, draping the cloth over a bar. "Being forced into the middle of something doesn't make it about you."

Sometimes Dime had a retort for Ella's comments, but that one actually struck her. Events couldn't be separated from the pyrsi who lived through them. It *was* about her now, even if it was about others as well. She felt like Ella would understand that.

"Ok," Dime tried again, "whatever's going on in Lodon, it's because the fairies showed up there. And the fairies showed up there, for some reason, because of me." The fact that it was *Dime* they'd tried to find was why she pyrsonally needed to find the High Seats and confront him. "It's all connected."

"Feels that way," Ella said with a shrug. "But you do know you're attempting to waltz in on the most powerful Fo-ror, the one who tried to capture you? I mean, I'm just checking."

Did Ella think Dime hadn't thought this through a thousand times over the past two days and nights? "Sure, I'm going to where he wanted me in the first place, but I'm going on *my* terms. Not his. That's different. Second, maybe he's not the most powerful Fo-ror."

"Oooh," Ella teased.

"Not me. Suzanne."

"What?" Ella's face froze, and Dime worried she'd gone too far.

"Suzanne. If it weren't for her, you wouldn't be here with the knowledge that you have. You wouldn't have found me or stopped me back at Lodon. You wouldn't have told me things I'll need to know and given me things I'll need. I don't know what I can do, but if I can do anything, it'll be because of Suzanne. Because she chose her own path."

"I need some kindling," Ella mumbled, grabbing a curved wood staff and starting down the tower's spiral staircase without another look.

Well, it was true. Ella and Suzanne, living here together, not caring that the world said they couldn't . . . it moved Dime. If they could be bold, Dime could as well.

And that included the fact that she was *not* a Fo-ror, or at least not *just* one. She didn't know what she was, but she had grown up among the Ja-lal. She knew them. She loved them. She'd married one. Her children were Ja-lal. Her life was Ja-lal. Maybe she was more than she'd realized, but no one was going to define her by what parts or abilities she had or didn't have.

Dime was defined by who she was.

Sipping her brew, Dime walked back over to Friend's window. She'd grown attached to the spiky plant, and now that she considered it, she'd never seen one similar. Friend's needles were not sharp like many in the surrounding woods, but plump, rounded at the ends. It didn't literally respond to her, but she felt an energy from it, as though it did.

A small glass contraption protruded from the soil at one end. She'd seen them in midcity shops. A bulb held extra water, so if Ella left for a while, Friend would have a few turns of wet soil.

Noticing her wrist compass as she ran her hand over the plant, she inspected the little metal needle. It had seemed to stop working when she was staying with the newts in what they called the Beds, but now it pointed sur again, at least somewhat sur. She hoped it was working. The going-away present from her Circlemates had been given to her just before this whole ordeal had begun; she felt connected to it now.

In fact, other than her utility knife and a couple other simple tools that had been in her old work jacket, the compass was one of only three things she had from her own home. Another being two small stone dice, a gift from her friend, Ador, less than a take before the fairies had burst in. And, of course, her diamond pendant.

Ella had told her diamonds were sacred to the Fo-ror, and the uncut one she possessed was of immeasurable value, not just for its size but quite literally, as the Fo-ror despised and did not use currency. Dime clutched the octagonal pendant protectively before tucking it back under her shirt. Another mystery to unravel.

She rinsed out the brew cup and set it on a drying cloth. The view through the window caught her eye, as it often did. Sol's light bounced and danced over the needled trees and hanging vines. Though part of Ja-lal lands, she wondered how many knew such a treasure existed here, at the wesside edge of Sol's Reach.

Probably very few.

Compelled to feel the fresh breeze on her face, she padded down the spiral stairs, admiring the fit of the new boots on her feet.

Pushing open the smoothly carved door, Dime stepped into the light. A breeze smelling of sap and wood and dirt tickled her nose, and squips bounced from branch to branch. Ella was walking back up the hill, her curved stick in one hand and a bundle of small kindling tucked under the opposite arm.

"Did I upset you?" Dime asked. Not always having the best read on pyrsi's reactions, she'd learned long ago that sometimes it was best to just ask.

"No. Here, look at this." Ella set the sticks next to the stone tower wall and pointed over to a tree. "Not too close."

Dime gasped. A nest was built into the crook of a large branch, each layer woven as though by expert hands. It wound over the contours of the tree, asymmetrical yet elegant in each turn. She'd never seen anything like it. Birds nested in the towers of Lodon, but only in small walkside trees, or wherever they could find a nook amongst the walls and ledges.

"Creatures are good at different things. And when you encourage those things, and otherwise let them be, they create pure beauty."

Dime didn't bother to object to the ch'pyrish parable, as if she weren't into her Gamh. She did consider that, like this nest, Ella had lived here a long time. It must be lonely, though. Dime knew better than to ask why she didn't return to the city. Maybe if Dime lived here, she wouldn't either. But, still.

"I hope that we are friends," Dime offered.

"Well, I'd hope so too. I mean, what does it take?"

The two fe'pyrsi laughed together at the edge of the old woods while the bird with the elaborate nest chattered down at them and the trees' needles shook above like a thousand little rattles in the breeze.

"I can't thank you enough for all you've done for me." Dime really couldn't.

"I told you, buy me a ferm." She made a little drinking motion with one hand, as if to punctuate.

Dime smirked. "It would have to be one super ferm at this point."

"Excellent! I have no lack of faith."

A feeling overtook her. "Would you accept a hug?" Dime would have to stop acting like an awkward ch'pyr around the older fe'pyr. No wonder she got so many lectures.

Ella moved forward and wrapped her arms around Dime, lingering as her hands pressed into her back and Dime leaned in, her chin lightly brushing Ella's shoulder. The warmth of the embrace comforted Dime. They stepped back apart.

"Could I ask for a promise?"

"Sure . . ." Dime hesitated to say *anything*, but, well, what could she refuse this fe'pyr? "Anything."

"If you're in danger near here or up to the city, you'll let me know. Send up one of those flares, if you can. You'll give me a chance to help you. That . . . would mean a lot."

Dime just sort of stared, thinking about whether it was a promise she could keep.

Ella pressed her fingertips together. "Look, I'm just here, with my trees and the squips and Friend. And my memories— The Ja-lal and the Fo-ror, this has gone on too long. A connection will risk the Violence, they say." Ella paused. *"It is the Violence to keep us apart."* A pleading look entered her eyes. "Maybe . . . maybe you will help. Maybe I can help you."

Dime nodded. Perhaps it was the timing of their meeting, or perhaps more, but Dime felt a special connection to this fe'pyr. And it bothered her to leave her alone again, she realized.

"I promise," she said. She stared up at the large bird nest, thinking of what else she could say as an appropriate departure. When she looked back, Ella was gone.

"Goodbye, Friend," she whispered, with a wave to the second-level window.

Unlike her previous feelings of relief and homecoming at reaching the dry and magnificent foothills of Sol's Reach, Dime felt a sadness as she passed out of the old woods' boundaries and back onto the tufted hills.

She'd fallen in love with the old woods, yet Lodon had always been her home. This was disorienting, as she couldn't live in the trees and in the city all at once. She reminded herself, home was the pyrsi she loved—and the physical items that connected them to her. Wherever those pyrsi were, and the objects and places around them: *that* was home. She tried to believe it.

Glancing back in the direction of Lodon, Dime almost turned around. Her longing to see her family had only intensified with time. Being told they were safe wasn't the same as seeing for herself. She wished she could talk to Dayn. Ask what he thought. Except she knew— he'd tell her to trust her instinct. And her instinct took her to Pito.

With a deep sigh, Dime turned away from Lodon again. And walked. "I'll come back," she whispered.

She'd thought about finding a toothcar, but had decided against it. A rental would be too risky; she couldn't say when she'd bring it back or how. And a purchase would be wasteful; she'd have to borrow substantially more of Ella's unsigned notes, even if she had enough to spare, and then perhaps leave the car waiting at the cliff.

Perhaps more to the point, she needed to avoid pyrsi as much as possible until she understood what was going on.

It sounded like an understatement: *what was going on.* How else was she supposed to describe a general crumbling of a historical truce between two species, combined with the revelation, after almost half of a lifetime, that she was biologically one and culturally the other? Oh, with both governments out searching for her. And meanwhile, she'd befriended some newts.

She'd continue to tooth with the *going on* description, then.

Dime began a very long walk across Sol's Reach. As her compass now seemed to just point whichever way she was going, she ignored it and relied instead on the shadows.

Pointing in the direction Ella had told her to travel, Dime's path traced a stark angle to her previous journey sur. That one had started in Lodon and taken her to the wesside of the Great Cliff, where she'd tumbled down what she now knew to be one of the less severe sections. This time, she'd started not so far wes of Lodon, and was headed to the center of the cliff.

She wasn't returning through the Crossing. Passing through the strange settlement would have made her nervous now, thinking pyrsi might be on the look for her. But that wasn't the main reason she aimed instead at the cliff's center.

Pito, the fairies' large city, was located in the center of Ada-ji, essentially directly sur of Lodon. Lodon rested about as far from the Great Cliff as it could, while Pito sat close against it. Dime liked taking scenic routes, but not so far out of the way as the Crossing would have taken her. And surely descending the cliff was much more pleasant with gear—and on one's feet.

Her destination felt absurd when she continued to think about it. The Heartland was an unapproachable place—a dangerous far-away land. Yet, one could reach it over the course of a day or a night, even from as far as she was now, and even on foot. Yet, pyrsi either never ventured to try, or those who did never talked about it. Maybe something one was taught xyr whole life wasn't so easy to see around. Which became downright sinister when those messages were orchestrated. She took a breath and rested her hand over her necklace. Since no one was here to see, she flipped it out, over her shirt.

While discussing the cliff, Ella had confirmed the hushed rumors Dime had dismissed these many cycles, that there were caves of diamonds in the center of Ada-ji. The Great Cliff, Ella said, held entrances to them, at the edge of Pito itself. Instead of being a secret, as they were to the Ja-lal, they were known and discussed openly amongst the Fo-ror.

Yet they were not visited so openly. The Seats maintained full control over the caves, and no pyr was allowed even to approach them without authorization. No pyr would try.

Dime now understood that, unlike the hemsa enforcement of Lodon, in Pito they subscribed to a technique called *arrest*, where pyrsi could be taken and secluded away, perhaps in separate homes. She wasn't sure about the details.

She also wasn't sure if, when she arrived in Pito, they'd continue with her arrest. Even Ella didn't have a full sense of their laws. Suzanne had never lived in Pito, only visited, and much like in Sol's Reach, Ella had explained, rules were stricter in the city.

But Dime had spent a good part of a career as an Intel agent, even if that had turned into much more managerial work in the towers than she'd expected. Those cycles had given her skills, also. She was clever and knew her way around pyrsi. And, she admitted, she was feeling stubborn.

Ma'Ferala, as Ella had called the High Seat—well, they'd both see how this was going to go.

Maybe Dime should have been more scared. Based on the fairy tales of her youth, she would have been. But she'd seen their faces, their very pyr-like expressions. She'd seen fear in their eyes. Nervousness. Relief. All in the short time they'd faced each other.

Or maybe, Dime had already overcome her own fear. Recognizing the fleeting nature of her life, she'd left her career. She no longer had failure to fear; she'd already done that.

The Violence? They'd already done that to her too.

She trudged on.

Climbing was as familiar as stone to the norside Ja-lal.

And with Sol setting across the horizon, Dime knew she'd want to hurry. Perhaps she'd not hurried enough on the long journey from Ella's tower, but it was nice to feel like herself again. To walk in Sol's warm light. And to think.

No, she'd be fine.

She peered over a dip in the cliff's edge, her stomach turning a bit at the enormity of the drop before her. Unlike the sloped and wooded cliff she'd tumbled down on the wesside, she now gazed at a chilling wall of rock that descended into little green treetops poking up from far below—the forest of the Undergrowth. Not fully sheer, the uneven face held small ledges and outcrops. If she were careful, she could lower herself in stages.

A stone bumped from her toe and bounced down the cliff's side, its cracking noises dulling with each bounce. Dime shuddered.

Climbing spikes and ropes in hand, Dime neither dallied nor rushed. She jostled each spike to make sure it was secure before pulling her rope over it, and she kept her focus steady as her feet found each hold, keeping space between her torso and the rough rock face. Section by section, she descended with caution, and did not panic when darkness fell.

Which was to say, on the side of the cliff, it did not set. It fell.

Dime took a calming breath, remembering what Ella had said. Despite a lifetime of relying on lamps at the slightest darkness, Dime's eyes were Fo-ror. They seemed to naturally adjust to the dark, even if just a small amount. She didn't know if they would have adjusted more with Fo-ror use and training early on, but she was glad for whatever help they offered. After about a bell, she was near the bottom, able to make out the silhouettes of trees around her.

Like feeling for the end of a staircase in the dark, she tapped around, one foot and then the other, searching for another ledge, another drop. Finally finding nothing but flat rock, she collapsed to a seat. As her eyes continued to adjust, the trees formed around her. Above her.

Dime was back in the Heartland.

She squinted down at her compass. It was jumping like a squip again, the thin needle bouncing in all directions. Maybe the devices didn't work closer to the Heartland, but it hadn't been right when she left Ella's either. Sighing, she unclipped it and folded it into a pouch. When she made it back to Lodon—no one could keep her out forever—she'd take it to a repair shop for a look.

So, it seemed, she'd need to find this city on her own. Fortunately, Ella had said it was similar in size to Lodon, so she only had to not miss it entirely.

Lowering herself down the massive cliff had been tiring, and

Dime had already given up on fear. As the trees took shape in the darkness around her, she moved to a clearing to find a place to sleep. She slept well and woke rested. Not hearing anything but the sounds of nature, she lit a fire. Calmed by the snaking patterns of the wafting smoke, she unpacked a meal and a filter bag to make some brew, once she found a source of water.

Dime worried about the net she had encountered near the cliff when she was further wes. It might extend here, as well. Yet, a short walk led her to a bubbling brook with plenty of water to drink, clean, and steam a good brew.

Enjoying a slow meal and an extra cup of the brew, she absorbed the sounds and smells of the forest. As before, the forest did not operate in subtlety. It whirred and clicked and raced around her, fully alive in the darkness. In the distance, a large branch fell, and she listened to it cracking its way to the ground, its final fall echoing through the tree trunks.

Packing to leave, she set off again into the night. No net hindered her path as she walked through the damp, musky forest, her new boots snug against her comfortable feet.

She now understood why Ella had insisted on oiling the canvas, layer by layer over the course of multiple treatments. In Sol's Reach, one mostly worried about what sort of rock was under xyr feet. Here, sudden patches of mud, or even gurgling puddles, popped out of nowhere as the terrain varied from step to step. It shocked Dime every time, and the chattering squips got to hear some new words as she plunked her feet from the mud.

It would be impossible not to marvel at the trees as she walked. Though she was trying her best to maintain her declared fealty to the mountainous beauty of Sol's Reach, she already knew that her perspective had changed: that she would mourn living in a place not surrounded by living, towering beings. Their leaves whispered as she walked, giving life to a whole system of birds and bugs and critters that leapt and bounded and crawled.

And the sounds of night birds in the trees—she closed her eyes just to take it all in. Music was Dime's passion. She thanked each bird for the chorus of harmony and dissonance that filled her ears as she walked in what she calculated to be the general direction of Pito.

She took her time over what felt like at least a couple of bells, maybe three counting her stops to rest. It was hard to tell, as the dancing night shadows gave no indication. With deliberate steps, Dime took care not to injure herself. Paying close attention to the geography, she also took notes—for future reference, or in case she accidentally doubled back.

Other sounds emerged. Percussive noises, calls, *voices*. Paths formed through the trees, confirming she was going the right way. She took the cloak from her bag and draped it over her head, shaking so it fell down over her backpack and trying to ignore the discomfiting feel of fabric against her scalp.

She quieted, watching her steps and noting and tracking each sound with the instinct of an agent, ingrained through her training. Strangely, she saw no homes. No structures. Yet she followed the clear sounds of civilization, confused why they hadn't come into view. She assessed each path, choosing those that were wider and more worn.

The rush of water caught her attention. Not the wild sound of a stream, but a large amount of water, similar to an overflow ravine in Lodon. This was pyr-made and would lead to a city. Soon, she found it, an unassuming river.

Not entirely unnatural, it ran through the soil, but it had been deepened and reinforced to form a smooth passage for the water to run downward toward the city. Glad for the cover of the trees— nothing felt open here in the forest—she crept along the banks.

A noise from above startled her, and she stopped, clinging to the side of a wide trunk. Her fallacy realized, she gasped at the massive structures above her.

They live in the trees.

Now, Ella had discussed their homes, some of the terms, and concepts she thought Dime should know. Yet she had not directly explained that the buildings were not towers at all, but structures built to weave through the shapes of the trees themselves, their foundations nestled into the largest branches.

Perhaps Ella assumed she knew.

And then she saw them: fairies, zapping to and fro, their large wings flapping like butterflies in an arboretum. They, as oblivious to her down here creeping in the mud as she had been to them. Lights glowed from the tree tops—not with the flames of lamps, but a soft glow, unfamiliar to her. It was critical, then, that she continue to stay invisible, here in the brush.

A moan sounded from the side.

Sidling around the trunk, she saw a fairy, retching on the ground. Xyr wings smacked against the dirt with force and a lack of control. Stones scraped against xyr arms.

No one was around, and the fairies above ignored or did not see xyr plight.

Dime glanced in all directions. No one was here. No one would see her.

"Hey," she whispered. "Hey, can I help?"

"You can killing leave me the kill alone," the pyr snapped, before turning to xyr side and vomiting across the dirt. Dime noted with disgust xyr proximity to the canal, with its clean-looking water.

"You can move away from the water before you do that again."

To her surprise, the pyr laughed.

"Where are you from?" xe asked, rolling onto xyr side with tiny pebbles lodged into xyr face.

"What?" Dime felt uneasy, for the pyr could see her now, see her tattoos. Though, she figured, xe was in no state to give her problems.

"Your accent; it's so weird. Kill, you have brute lines on your face. Holy Sha, I'm tripping, aren't I?" Xe clawed into the soil, moving away from the creek, where xe vomited again.

Tripping. Tzetz.

The symptoms clicked into place. Dime had little experience

with the addictive substance; anyone involved was shooed out of the high city with a hemsa and no incentive to come back.

She crouched down. "I'm a Ja-lal. Name's Fe'Dime. I guess this is how I speak." Dime was expecting the fairy's smooth pronunciation and tilted vowels this time. Having no context who she was, Dime's speech must sound oddly clipped.

Her hood still in place, she looked into the pyr's eyes. They were red and tired. "You can decide whether or not you want to believe that, but neither of us needs to let anyone know about any of this. I, uh, is there any way I can help you?"

Dime backed away a little, for the scent of the vomit was not pleasant.

"Ma'Uchitar. I'm a loser." He tried to peer through her hood. "Ja-lal. Sure. My parents always told me I'd end up taken by the brutes. Sorry I told you to kill off. Seem nice enough."

With that, he crawled another measure away and threw up again. Collapsing back onto the ground, his arms shook against his gray robe. A little whimper escaped him.

It seemed like a robe, a garment for wearing around home. The other fairies she'd seen had similar clothes. So, then, they wore robes in the open. His was covered in an intentional patchwork, with what she suspected would be pretty colors had they not been dragged through the dirt and grime. His hair—and yes, he had hair—was white, which she now knew to be her own natural color. Though, unlike the thin stubble Dime had shaved off, Uchitar's long hair was tied into a large knot over his head.

Even collapsed in the dirt, it had a distinct style to it. Then she noticed there were even bands of hair across his eyebrows. *Eyebrow hair!* Did he have to style them, or did they just stay that length?

"Um, Uchitar? Can I get something for you?" Again, Dime wished she knew more about medical assistance. For her older child, Luja, it was a passion. But, Dime realized with another pang of longing for her family, Luja was not here. Dime thought about what was in her bag that might help him. She was nervous to make him worse.

"He needs water," a voice said.

Dime jumped back and clutched the hood around her face as another fairy flapped xyr wings, carrying xem over the creek to where Uchitar lay.

Xe set down a glowing stone, which lit the area around them. "Don't be scared if you're new. I'm Fe'Volana. Pyrsi know me here. No ties to the Seats. No judgment. Just help, as I can offer it. Please, stay."

Now this fairy was extraordinary. With the light gray skin of a mid-Bakh, she bore no tattoos, something Dime was accepting really was normal here. Her hair—Dime also resolved to stop being surprised by hair—swung down from her head in thin braids, like rope. White, like Uchitar's. She wondered why the others had darker hair. Theirs had looked dyed like fabric, so maybe it was.

Volana's robes were made of a neutral fabric without much tailoring, but nothing about her was plain. Long strips of lace and ribbon, scraps, perhaps, were stitched to her robes, giving her the grace of a dancer as she turned. She appeared to be far along in a pregnancy, and the ribbons hung from her protruding middle, swaying over the ground.

Ignoring Dime now, Volana took a copper bowl to the creek, dipping it in and returning to poor, twitching Uchitar.

"May I touch you?" she asked. When Uchitar gave a little grunt, Volana poured the water onto a cloth, dabbing it around his mouth.

"You can help," she said to Dime. "It doesn't transfer."

Following Volana's lead, Dime helped pull Uchitar to a seat, and the fairy tipped the bowl to his quivering lips, allowing him to drink in small sips. "You can't hurl in the creek, friend. You got close that time. What happened to the flask I gave you?"

"Gave it away."

Volana sighed. "You can't win. You give them anything to stay their pain, they give it away for more tzetz." She glanced up at Dime. "Do you use?"

She supposed the question wasn't odd here, but given Dime's

cloaked face, and raised back that probably didn't pass for the right shape of wings, Dime felt surprised at the fe'pyr's lack of other questions. And Dime realized she was, right now, very face-to-face with a fairy.

"No," she answered. "I'm sorry. I need to go."

"Be well," Volana said, helping Dime lower Uchitar back onto the ground. Dime scanned around her, determining the safest path, as three fairies swept down from the skies, landing just in that direction. Detailed robes, colorful hair pulled into elaborate shapes—she guessed they held some rank or class. She was grateful for the dark, a heavy darkness in the cover of the forest once away from Volana's light, and reminded herself that they could see no better than she. She stepped backward, as far as she dared without checking what was behind her.

"Look, the cleaning pyr can't stop cleaning the garbage!" One of the fairies laughed. Volana stood tall, her white braids swinging into place and the copper bowl cupped in her hands over top of her rounded middle. The light emanating from the stone cast her in a spotlight amidst the darkness, and Dime was transfixed by the image.

"Sha's waves," one said, making an unfamiliar gesture. "Xe was puking in the creek. That's disgusting."

"That's a crime, you know," another added. "Guess we should go get a marshal. Give xem some time in the caves. Xe can puke there, then Volana can go clean it up. Marshal! Marshal!" Xe mock-called the words but not loudly enough to really call anyone.

"Leave him alone, please," Volana said. "You've had your tease, now fly on."

Dime noticed the third fairy hadn't said anything. This didn't impress her; hanging out with jerks was no accomplishment. So, apparently fairies were just regular pyrsi. It was settled now. Maybe she'd been hoping for more.

The jerk fairies were positioned right where she wanted to go. She could cross the creek, which would certainly draw attention to her lack of flight. She could turn around and head back the way she'd traveled, which would draw attention to her back. Or she could stand here like an odd statue and hope they . . . what was it? Flew on.

"Whoa. What's that?" A fairy pointed right at Dime. "Is xe carrying another one on xyr back or something?"

"Look," another said. "What's wrong with xyr wings?" They stopped laughing.

They hadn't used any valence, that she could see. She didn't know if they would. Yet, Ella said the Violence was just as abhorred here as in Sol's Reach, so her worst danger was capture.

Capture.

It was why she was here, right? Volana looked as if she were about to speak. *No, she can't be involved in this.* She straightened up.

On my terms.

"I am here to see the High Seat. I'm submitting to his call for my arrest."

Remembering Ella telling her about Suzanne's lack of fear in talking to the Light, she added one last detail. "I will speak to no pyr except to the High Seat himself."

Volana dropped her bowl, hitting Uchitar in the side. She squealed, leaning down to check on him.

"Marshal!" one of the jerks called, this time meaning it. "Marshal!" Xe flew off, screaming. Xyr companions stayed, glancing at each other and avoiding Dime's gaze.

She felt a little light-headed, and reminded herself to breathe evenly.

Other fairies swept in from above, hearing the commotion. Soon, Dime was surrounded by curious onlookers. Trying to keep her attention on the pyr facing her, she couldn't absorb all the detail, but it was impossible not to stare at the pyrsi who surrounded her, eclipsing any sense of style purported by the Ja-lal.

Ja-lal wore tailored lines, bold adornments. Well placed juxta-positions of color. Fo-ror already surpassed this with their sea of iridescent wings, covering every shade of blue, indigo, and violet.

Their hair rose and fell in sculpted shapes. Elegant robes swayed around them, cut to allow their wings freedom of movement. Jewels, chains, and baubles reflected the light of Volana's glowing stone.

Seeing the growing crowds, she thought that *maybe* she should have done this a subtler way.

And they were all watching her. Whispering. No, she couldn't let them see her running away, fleeing into the night. No more of that. Yet, she held her cards as she could, keeping her cloak and hood in place. The crowd grew, pyr by pyr, but no one approached her, even as Volana wrapped Uchitar around her like a huge limp sack and did her best to drag him back into the trees, out of sight of the arriving marshals. Dime wished she could help, but at least her presence kept all eyes off them.

Dime assumed two fairies to be marshals as soon as they flew toward her. They wore plain robes and small pins, of a different shape than she'd seen—and these without the sparkle of diamonds. Dime spoke before they reached her, wanting to control the interaction as best she could. "The Seats have called for my arrest."

The marshals scanned the ground around where Dime stood, sniffing in disgust. "Look, pal, the *Seats* don't call for the arrest of pushers. And what's with the weird voice? Someone's got a little fancy with xemself. Just come along with us."

"If you'll promise me you'll take me to the Seats. No other judge or forum; it must be the Seats."

"Promise you," xe sputtered. "Or what?"

Dime approached, taking deliberately slow steps, and leaned toward the marshal, whispering close to xyr ear. "A secret? I am a Ja-lal. Look at the shape of my cloak, it's not quite right for wings, is it? My accent. I can show you the markings on my face." She paused.

"I will speak to the High Seat myself, or you will be the one to explain to him why you let a whole crowd of onlookers witness the return of the Ja-lal to Pito. Again. I want your promise that I will go directly to the Seats. Also, we'll need to walk, so, however you want to handle that with this crowd. But first, before they leave, you promise."

Pushing her dramatic flair maybe a little, Dime held her face near his for one extra-long stride, then backed away, tugging the hood forward another time. Xe held up a hand, giving xyr partner a look that indicated to stay back.

"I promise I will take you to the Seats." It was said low, so only Dime could hear. Ella had told her the strength of Fo-ror honor. She hoped it would hold. "Sha, pal," xe added.

The marshal waved at the crowd, raising xyr voice so they could all hear. "Everyone, leave the area. This prisoner is unstable, and we need space to deal with xem. Shoo. Go on." The crowd lifted back into the air, clearly not wanting trouble with a marshal. Xe whispered something to xyr partner, and after a quick but intense conversation, the partner flew off.

From where Volana and Uchitar rested in the darkness of the trees, Dime realized they had been staring this whole time at her back. Hoping the gesture conveyed here, she fanned her fingers behind her, in their direction. Then, toward the marshal, she fanned her fingers over her heart. "I am ready."

The marshal still looked stunned. Xe glanced again at her shoulders, then jerked his head away. "Normally I'd introduce myself, but to be honest, I want nothing to do with you. Don't show me that stuff you talked about, and let's just go. It's a long walk."

"Thank you," Dime said.

Together, she and the uneasy marshal took a surreal hike through what she now understood were the underpinnings of Pito. A couple of times, pyrsi saw them, but recognizing the marshal, flew away.

Dime wished she could take in all the creaks and sounds she heard above her and see what sort of dwellings could be built among the trees, but the drawn hood blocked her view of anything but the path in front.

The marshal's breaths were heavy to her side. She wondered if walking was more tiring for fairies. "Do you need to rest?" she asked. "I won't leave. You have my word."

"No, thanks. I'd rather get this over with. You can understand that."

Dime smiled, though xe couldn't see it.

The agent in her tickled at this opportunity—a long walk with a government official, and the ability to ask questions that might help her later. Two things stayed her. First, the marshal was clear xe wanted nothing to do with her, yet xe was honoring her request, which could get xem in trouble. She wanted xem to know she respected both aspects of that, to keep xem on her side. Second, and more importantly, she'd declared—wisely or not—that she'd only communicate with the High Seat. Now that she'd played that card, she wasn't ready to discard it.

It felt like at least a bell that they walked together in silence, the marshal slowing as they went. Rather than worry about what the next turns might bring or watch the dull dirt path bounce before her, she listened to the sounds of Pito. Water, wind, and a chorus of bird calls around her—forest sounds. Creaking, flying, and distant laughter above her—what she supposed were city sounds. For a while, the noise above grew louder and more chaotic, then, as the ground grew rockier under her boots, it grew quiet again.

After a lifetime of using her senses in full, Dime yearned for the hood to be off. She understood that the marshal didn't want to see. Many didn't. That said, she knew xe wouldn't forget her, whether or not xe'd seen her face. For that, she didn't know whether she was sorry.

As it appeared the fairies all lived above the ground, or at least did in Pito, she did not expect to be led to an outdoor corridor at ground level, not far from a sloping wall of rock. A guard, for she knew nothing else to call xem, emerged under an archway, blocking their passage.

"Your Honorous, this pyr was found downcreek saying xe had an arrest decree and xe needed to see the High Seat."

The guard rolled xyr eyes, tapping a wood staff against the stone path. "A pyr says xe wants to see the High Seat and you take xem here? Seriously? What is your name?"

"Your Honorous," the marshal dropped to a whisper, "I swear to you on Sha's ways, I want no part of this. Xe said more. More I can't repeat. Please. Please, I beg you, take the pyr. Let me leave."

Dime watched the guard's eyes flick with annoyance. Xe reached into a pocket in xyr robes, as if for a pen. Xe wasn't buying it.

"Burge," Dime offered, to get xyr attention. Angled so the marshal could not see but the guard could, Dime pulled her hood back on one side, allowing just a border of her vine tattoos to be visible in the nightlight. The guard's eyes widened.

"Promise you will not speak of it," the guard hissed to the marshal.

"I promise," the marshal whispered. "With your leave?"

"Go," xe returned. The marshal flew away without pause.

As if invited in, Dime walked on past the guard, under the arch and through the large open door behind xem. "This way?" she asked.

The guard gnarred behind her, but she could tell xe was following as she walked along a long, stone corridor, lit with more of the glowing stones and lined with carved statues. "Through there," xe directed as she reached a juncture. Dime obeyed. After several more turns, the adorned passageways ended, replaced by plain corridors, almost tunnels. Having imagined an elegant tower with a view of trees, she did not expect these long, dreary halls. Or the quiet. Or isolation.

Yet there was something stirring in this empty place, a feeling she could not describe. It made her uneasy, like an itch.

Her concern grew as she saw no paintings, no signs of office work. The air grew cool against her exposed hands. It was becoming clear she was not approaching any grand chambers. The walls were gray and brown, spotted with patches that looked like char, but hardened like they'd been there a long time.

Passing through an old-looking door, Dime stepped into the middle of a much wider corridor, brightly lit and extending to her left and right. Dime stopped cold, seeing the structures that lined it in both directions.

She'd seen cages before; Luja used them to transport wounded animals to the medical enclave. These cages were pyr-sized and cubical in shape. Each was formed by long, glimmering bars, and inside, rested stark furnishings: a round stool, a chair, a wide bed, and a tray-like table. A smaller cage connected to each in the back, shielding what appeared to be commodes. The large corridor—or long room, she supposed—smelled musty, but clean.

Dime's gut wrenched at this idea of confinement. Thinking of it had troubled her, but seeing it spun her mind into a state of fury. She fought every instinct to run.

Without anyone touching it, one of the cage doors swung open. *Valence.* Dime was still not used to the reality that fairy wings truly did hold mystic powers, but, she realized, she'd better get used to it fast.

For a moment, she considered refusing to enter. She didn't know if they would force her in anyway, or whether it would be wise to tempt them. Or, if not, whether she'd be less of a prisoner sitting here, in the middle of the floor. At least the cage held a chair.

Now was not the time for Dime to doubt her plan. She hadn't felt scared in her own small office in the towers; she imagined this as another. She stepped into the cage and the door closed in front of her. A small object flew from the guard's hands, glittering as it zipped into the area of the handle. She heard a click, and the object flew back again. Xe relaxed a quick moment and then left, the glittering key still in xyr grip.

They locked it! She knew what a cage was for, but it was different to sit in one than to be *locked* in one. Dime felt like the air had been taken from her lungs in the small space. Then, she considered what it must feel like to a fairy used to flying, and anger joined her anxiety. Each furnishing had more space between it than she was used to, and the ceiling lifted higher; she supposed that accommodated wings. Still, it was small. Stifling.

She sat in the chair, really just trying to acclimate to this confining space, trying to regain calm and resolve, to keep herself in control for when they returned.

After a while, a pyr walked into the room, wearing striped, orange robes, layered chains of glittering jewelry, and a large, rust-colored twist of hair. By xyr skin, xe was perhaps Dime's age. "Say your name," xe commanded.

"I will speak only to the High Seat," Dime responded. Still held by the anxiety of the small space and still wearing the dark hood and cloak, the arriving fairy brought her no additional fear. Instead, Dime grew annoyed.

The pyr paused. "I am Seat Fe'Dailawe. Perhaps you did not know. Why have you lied to our guard?"

Lied? Dime never lied. This infuriated her, beyond any annoyance. Yet she wouldn't be drawn in by a ruse. "I will speak only to the High Seat."

"If you are not lying," Dailawe said, "then whatever you were told is wrong. The Seats have issued no arrest for a Ja-lal. You should not have come here."

Dime was struck with a beat of panic in her heart. Had she come here for nothing? But the pin. The Fo-ror who'd burst into her home had been wearing the Seats' pin. No. Even if she were wrong about who had tried to take her, she was born a Fo-ror. She was still a Ja-lal, but that did not make her *not* a Fo-ror either. Her wings had been removed, stealing her heritage. Her history. Her ability to use valence as the others did.

For answers, she would speak to the High Seat. Which was even more relevant if this important pyr truly did not know.

"With proper respect to you, Seat Dailawe, I will speak only to the High Seat. And I will not say it again."

With that, Dime sat her backpack down on the floor. She removed her cloak, folded it, and tucked it into the bag's large side pocket. Taking a deep breath, she sat back in the small chair, closed her eyes, and waited.

A crack issued from the side, forcing Dime's eyes open again by reaction. A miniature light show exploded before her, filling the room with blue light. The Seat raised her hands to her sides, silhouetted against her wings. Bright azure bolts and sparks bounced between the stone walls, zapping around like festival fireworks, meant, she supposed, to impress her into speaking.

If this was meant to impress or even frighten her, perhaps Dailawe should have seen the fireworks Dayn and Ador had recently constructed. Dime had worried they'd blown up the tower skygarden.

Dailawe lowered her arms, stepping forward, as the room returned to its previous state. *A show of her valence, then. Fine.*

With a look that told Dailawe she'd have to do better than that, Dime closed her eyes again. This time, she focused on music. She remembered the little songs that she'd written during her long turns in the field, the fragments of longer pieces she'd not had the time to stitch together.

She relaxed into the fledgling tunes within her mind, blocking any sense of whether Dailawe continued to speak.

Dime may have even fallen into an uncomfortable half-sleep for a while. She stirred, rested but stiff. Standing, she stretched and looked around. A simple latch opened the pathway to the commode, which was as clean as she could imagine without the benefit of plumbing. Closing the smaller door again, she returned to her seat.

The guard, when xe returned, did not look happy to see her. Without words, xe unlocked the cage, again with the glittering key, and motioned for her to follow. Dime heaved the backpack on, but left the cloak in its pocket. The guard started at her tattooed head then glanced away, as if disgusted. Or embarrassed. Dime wasn't sure. She thought about talking to xem, but she'd drawn a line. She was staying behind it.

After a take or so of walking, xe transferred her to a second guard. This one, with the swagger to match it, wore the pin—the diamond pin of the Seats. Dime tried not to stare. She didn't recognize xem from the invasion into her home, or at least she didn't think so.

At this point, the drab tunnels opened into wood-paneled hallways, painted and carved like the most elaborate ferm hall in Lodon. Water ran, and metal clanged, and Dime had the distinct impression they were taking a back way to wherever they were going. The guard opened a wide door, and they stepped through together.

The expansive hall was the height of three or four levels. It smelled like cedar planks and a strong floral perfume. Large chandeliers of glowing stones provided ample light across the bright space. Despite the lofty ceiling, no pyrsi flew here, except a quick flutter to skip across more open portions of the hall. All stayed at floor level, their wings sometimes swaying, like flowers in a field.

Nine fairies stood, sat, or even perched upon huge chairs, arranged across a curved dais, faced at an angle from where Dime stood. Those who sat back had their wings spread wide and they leaned against them. Those sitting forward folded their wings behind, the two wings almost, but not quite, touching.

Each chair reminded her of a storybook throne, and each was decorated or upholstered differently, she supposed according to the wishes of each inhabitant. Small tables waited by each chair, some littered with papers and others pulled neatly to the side.

In the center of the arc, a fairy sat on a plain chair of dark hardwood, with rounded bars across its back, and a line of diamonds on its top. A cluster of white braids shifted at xyr side. Or, his, she realized. This must be Ma'Ferala, the High Seat.

She could have gazed at the elaborate beauty of this space for bells. She could have drunk in every detail, every rail and pillar. She could have memorized the elaborate embroidery of each gown, the wafting capes, and the towering hair. She could have stared forever.

But, it turned out, there was one Sol of an argument underway.

"Don't lecture me," Dailawe said with a bit of a growl. "It's not a coincidence! Not just the one, now, but both in our prison. At the same time? Are there others? This one swore not to talk except to the High Seat himself! I believed xem! Xe had a *truth* to xyr voice. Different than the other. Clearer. We need to know what's going on! Something is going *on*. This threatens our security!"

Both?

"Security threat?" another responded. "The security threat is taking some unknown brute into Chambers without vetting. Sha's *sacred hall*. Have you not studied history, Seat Dailawe? Should we return the Violence? Have xem do it for us? Watch our children die? What would you do? Would we—"

"Enough!" the fairy to Ferala's left growled. Dime shuddered. Even from afar, she did not like this pyr. Xyr sneering face, xyr drawn lips, xe rang of anger. Of bitterness. Xe wore a necklace of large metal beads, large diamonds set within each one, and xyr hair was pulled back with dark ribbons. "The brute will *not* be taken to Chambers; you will return it to prison and I will pyrsonally ensure its return to the Barrens."

Oh, that was not going to happen.

"Honorous High Seat Ferala," Dime called, her voice surprising her with its steadiness. She stepped forward. "I am Fe'Diamond of the Ja-lal, and I am responding to your order of arrest. I request a private audience to learn the nature of my crime."

Amidst the gasps and the clattering of dropped objects, all eyes first turned to Dime. And then to Ferala.

Ferala did not deign to look at her, but stared ahead, his mouth hidden behind dark gray fingers, covered in sparkling jewels. *Diamonds*. His fingertips pressed against his lips.

Dime glanced around the room, noting the shocked expressions, the gaping mouths. She noticed the way Ferala hid his own in his hands. His eyes stared ahead. Blank.

Understanding, Dime was now certain it was Ferala who'd tried to bring her here. But not like this. It was supposed to be in private. Not revealed here, in front of the others.

Yet what choice had she had? How could she sneak to find him, locked in a cage like a wounded squip? He could have communicated with her like a pyr, not sent his minions to take her in secret. He'd done this, not her.

"There are other matters to discuss!" she called. "*Other matters.* I will only wait so long. Know this." She stared directly at Ferala as she spoke. "I am willing to negotiate terms. Otherwise, the terms will be mine."

The angry Seat began to shout orders, but Ferala interrupted, talking over xem. "Dead caves. Now. No one is to have *any contact* with *either of them* until I decide how this is handled. And no news leaves this room. *None.* That is my decree." He slammed a staff onto the dais, with enough force that room crept to a silent stop.

Several pyrsi bowed low, while the Seat to Ferala's left just glared at him, a silent communication that Ferala would not return.

"Out, now," the guard whispered, not saying another word until they were back in the plain passages again. The waiting guard stood back up as the higher-ranking guard barked a few quick orders, turned on his toes, and left.

"Prisoner Fe'*Diamond*, huh? Seems I can't shake you." It was the same guard who had locked her in the first time. "I'm Guard Ma'Wayniam. We'll get along best if you don't bother me. Do you have any, uh, dietary needs?"

Dime assumed it was a standard question, but the way he asked it had a "what do you pyrsi eat" vibe that for some reason struck her as funny. She held back a smile. Given her situation, she wasn't sure why she was grinning so much.

"Call me Dime. Nothing serious, but I'm not the biggest fan of raw hullnut."

"Hullnut?"

"Not served here? Great, that's one point Fo-ror."

"Through here," he said with narrowed eyes, leading her back through the drab corridors, until they entered the wide corridor of cages again, though this time at one of the ends.

"So these are the dead caves?" Dime asked.

"I don't answer your questions."

A familiar voice wafted up the passage, gravelly but with a sultry edge. Dime tripped over her feet as Wayniam noted her shock. "Holy Sol," the voice continued, "is that really Agent Dime? You tell me right now that's Agent Dime."

Wayniam gritted his teeth as they walked toward the third cage, the one occupied by the unexpected voice.

"Know her?" He pointed into the cage.

Still stunned by what she thought she'd heard but unsurprised now by anything, this required quick thought. Maybe she shouldn't have ticked Wayniam off on the way here; he was unlikely to grant her requests. Ok. A risk.

"No." Dime stopped in place. "No. I will not be anywhere near that pile of refuse. I demand you place me back where I was. I *order you*, Guard Wayniam."

Wayniam turned around with puckered lips, his knotted hair bouncing over his shoulders. "You order me, brute? Ok. How about this?"

The key zipped through the air as the neighboring door swung open. Trying not to let the ever-flying key throw her off, Dime pretended to pout and then gave the guard the angriest face she could muster as she walked in and sat down. The door slammed shut with a click and the tiny key zipped back into his hands. Dime set down her backpack and turned away, arms wrapped around herself.

Chuckling, Wayniam left.

Dime spun on the round stool. Through the bars of the neighboring cage, she wasn't sure what to expect of the fe'pyr, the best agent she had ever known. There she sat in the middle of her bed, with drawn-on tattoos, painted blue lips, and eyes as bright as she remembered. That gray skin, though. Dime's could not have grown that gray. She glanced at her hands. *Harm it.* "*Rock.* What the kill are you doing here?"

"Maybe you're dreaming," Rock said, giving her a wink.

"Anyway, nice move with Waynie there. He's not really terrible; just hates his job."

A long, long moment passed as Dime stared into the agent's eyes. With a grunt, she looked away.

"Good to see you, D," Rock chimed. "It's been *way* too long."

Interlude

A whistle sounded outside Keliaka's bungalow. From the back room, her ba'pyr let a shrill cry. "Hold on," she yelled at the window, "you're early!"

The delivery crew probably couldn't hear her from the ground, but it made her feel better to scold them. After all, it was low-class delivery shift, so who cared whether her cooking was interrupted? Who cared whether the ba'pyr's nap was cut short? Who cared that she received the same plain food every time, while the pyrsi she served at work ate fine, seeded pods and soft grain noodles?

The whistle sounded again.

She grabbed last delivery's bags and whisked through the curtain, to see four pyrsi lowering a delivery blanket to the ground below, covered in bags of produce and grain. She flew down to meet them.

"Keliaka. Three. Standard." The pyr read them off, not introducing xemself. They never introduced themselves. Just knew her name from the list.

"Here," she handed over the empty bags. "My ba'pyr is crying. May I fly back up? Could you set them on the walk?"

The pyr rolled xyr eyes. "We've got a whole route ahead of us and two out sick. We'll leave them here. We trust you'll get to them soon." Another pyr unloaded three full bags, setting them off in the grass. "Be well," xe offered with a smile.

"Thank you," Keliaka said. "Most kind." After all, it did no good to irritate the delivery pyrsi. She didn't think they'd do anything to her delivery, but less enthusiasm she didn't need. "Sha's blessings," she added.

"See you next time." The pyrsi flew into the air, each holding a rope that wove through the edges of the blanket.

Her child screamed louder as she flew each bag up from the ground into the kitchen. "I'll be there soon!" she called.

Once the bags were on the table, she changed her child's wrap and then cuddled the little bundle against her chest with one arm. With her free arm, she pulled the items out of the bags and put each away.

"Do you know," she said, "that when I was a ch'pyr, I saw a medic once. Ve made my breathing better. I was so grateful; I wanted to be a medic. There is no pyr in the world who helps others more than that. And Sha told me I would be one, then I could help pyrsi too. Then your Ga-pa explained to me that I was not a medic. I was a server. My Da-da was a server. And so was I. I could serve the high class, just as he did. As he does," she corrected. "And that's where I met your Da-da. He's a wonderful server."

"I don't mind serving food," she continued as the ba'pyr began to settle. "But I'd rather help pyrsi heal." Keliaka stopped, a pang of guilt arresting her. Ba'pyrsi could hear. It didn't matter how young one was, a parent should not speak this way. Like any whimsy, any fantasy, it was best kept in its place.

Inside.

"We are servers," she said, pouring the new barley into the sack, too tired to reshuffle it. "Someturn you'll be a server too. It's very nice; you meet the most interesting pyrsi."

Shoving the empty bags into a cabinet, Keliaka rested back onto the rocking stool, her wings relaxing behind her. She could take a few more minutes before she started the pots. The turns went by too quickly.

"Shh," she said. "Ma-ma's here. There's no reason to cry. Soon you'll be crawling and flying." Not quite ready to consider that, she pushed the thought aside. "And you can be whatever you want to be in your life." With a wicked laugh she knew no one else could hear, she added a last thought, for she could not speak this way again. "As long as it's a server."

Act 2

In the Dark

"**W**hat are you doing here?" Dime asked again. She blinked a few times. Rock was still there.

"Ok, you're asking *me*," Rock said, twirling something in her fingers, "like you just hang out in fairy prison? Didn't know that about you."

Yes, this was Rock, alright. Never the first to offer information. Well, she wasn't going to waste time in some standoff with one of the smartest pyrsi she'd ever met. If she couldn't trust Rock, she wasn't interested in the game.

"I quit the Circles a few turns back." She counted. "Six and a half, actually." The invaders had arrived during the day, and this was the seventh night since. It felt like longer.

"I know," Rock answered, pulling her knees up to her chest. "Then the fairies came to Lodon to get you. Some pyrsi say you joined them. Others say you were captured. I knew about this place. Realized some things. Decided to find you."

"You didn't do very well?"

Rock grinned.

Harm it. "Ok, you found me. But, you're already locked in, what did you call it? Prison? I'm so unimpressed."

Rock leaned back with an even more smug grin.

Oh, kill that. "Ok. You meant to get captured. Which means you probably have a way back out. Which means there is way, way, more to this story."

"Oh, there is more to both of our stories, it seems. Glad you caught my vibe with Waynie, by the way. I was hoping you'd get it. Makes it so much easier if we can just talk right here. You always were quick on your feet."

Rock ended the thought with an awkward silence. Dime was not going to let this get awkward. There was no reason for it to get awkward. She could barely believe Rock was actually here. She gave the fe'pyr another glance. *It's really her.*

Dime couldn't deny feeling a little disoriented. The last time they'd parted, she'd just assumed they'd cross paths again—that effect of being young when everything feels permanent. But they hadn't. And, now, here they were.

"Hey, can we just talk about it?" Dime stumbled a bit on the words. "I mean, so much has happened since then. I haven't even seen you in, what, nine cycles? We were just barely into our Bakh then. It was like a lifetime ago." It was; she'd grown so much since then.

To her relief, Rock offered a warm smile. "*You* were barely into your Bakh. Don't remind me of my age. Anyway, just seeing you again, kind of a shock. You know? I'm over it. Anyway, nice family you've got. Two kids?"

The idea that Rock knew about her family was so Rock it didn't even disturb her. Rock kept tabs on everything, but with unflinching ethical boundaries. Dime had admired that. She started to relax. "Yeah, they're the best. Ji'Luja is nine, or 'almost ten' as ve says it. Fe'Tum is seven."

"Wow. A child in vis Bakh."

"Almost in vis Bakh." Dime corrected with a chuckle. "And in case you're working out the timeline, yes, Luja was a ba'pyr back then. We didn't meet ver until ve was two. Ve's so grown up now—working to be a medic, trying to get an apprenticeship in the enclaves. Won't have a problem; ve's so dedicated. Tum is making her way through school. Watch out when she decides what she's going to do."

"They sound like their mother."

"No," Dime replied, wishing she were more like her children. "They'll be better. They'll make a difference. I've—"

As Rock stared off down the passage, Dime snuck one long look at the fe'pyr, trying to believe it had truly been so long. Rock wore a sleek midnight blue shirt and pant set, trimmed with touches of pewter gray, and probably lined inside and out with pockets and small tools. She had the same odd look to her Dime remembered, even now with her wiser eyes and darker skin.

Committed to her art, Rock had no tattoos that were visible with standard clothing. To keep pyrsi from feeling too uncomfortable, she drew on highly-realistic markings with cosmetic paint, often adding, as she had now, a thick line under her eyes. That, Dime knew, was just for effect. Pyrsi weren't sure who they were dealing with, and Rock liked it that way. She was surprised Rock got away with it. All of it. No one had made a law about needing visible tattoos, because no one considered not having them. Except Rock.

Who was more beautiful than she'd ever been. Dime wasn't going to deny that, and she didn't think Dayn would begrudge her the observation. Yet, despite Rock's constant game face, from which she distracted pyrsi with her bold, blue lips, Dime sensed there was a sadness to her. It was palpable.

"So, uh, which did you think?" Dime asked.

Rock glanced over.

"I mean, whether I was captured or whether I joined them. The Fo-ror."

"Oh, I knew you weren't part of some conspiracy. Besides, I talked to your spouse. He said he didn't know where you were. I knew you wouldn't leave him like that."

The idea of Dayn talking to Rock felt strange, not that she was uncomfortable with it, just more like . . . separate worlds colliding. Those turns in the field were a long time ago. Dime had moved on.

Rock shifted in place. "Anyway, Wayniam won't be back for a while. I'll keep an ear out. Might as well get comfortable."

"Sure, thanks." Dime wasn't going to get too comfortable here, though of course Rock didn't know she'd sort of . . . scolded . . . the High Seat. Dime knew she should tell Rock about that, but she was feeling a little overwhelmed, honestly. Resolving to keep her things packed, she turned to her bag.

As she checked to make sure everything was still secure, she realized she hadn't put balm on her arms for a while. She rummaged a little before finding the small jar. Taking the cloak from the side pocket to work it down into the bag's bottom, she paused for a moment.

"Why'd they let me keep this?"

Rock peered through the bars. "A cloak? Eh. No threat. First, you're in a diamond cage, so you couldn't get out, even if you had valence."

"A diamond cage? I don't see any diamonds. Oh." She understood, running her hands along a bar and pulling them away at a small spark. "There's diamond dust in the metal. Just like the ropes they use."

"Doesn't take very much of it, from what I understand, and there's piles of the stuff back in the caves. They can charge it up with valence; it's even tuned to the pyr who does it."

She perked up, curious about what Rock knew about fairy valence. Dime knew almost nothing.

Rock shook her head. "The valence stuff, it's too much for me to try and understand. I stick to regular Intel, like who pyrsi are and what they're up to.

"Anyway, cloak won't help you here. Doesn't even look like a fairy cloak; theirs are separated in back, with long scarves that flutter when they fly. They're fun to watch, when you get the chance. And, no, draping that sack over your backpack does not look like wings. It would just read as deceptive to the pyrsi here, and you *don't* want that."

Rock raised a finger and let it fall to point at Dime's bag. "On top of all that, fairies are even more serious about 'taking' than we are.

They'll throw you in a metal box, but they won't take your backpack. *That* would be the Violence.

"You want my opinion? Just be who you are. The Dime I know would stuff that cloak in a fabric donation bin and never look back."

Dime still couldn't believe any of this. "You're going to tell me how you know so much about fairies, right?" She was really cranking on this one. Dime had learned first-hand how the IC took to questions about the Fo-ror. The only time she'd brought them up, she'd been buried in paperwork for turns and never returned to the field.

So how in Ada-ji was Rock learning about them? It couldn't be her assignments. Last she'd heard, Rock had fallen from favor within the IC a couple of cycles back after a run-in with Atti. Who *hadn't* had at least one run-in with the dispatcher, in fairness, but rumor said it was a bad one.

She'd heard afterward the agent had been subdued by the leadership, given the same sort of uninteresting assignments they'd both had when starting out. Certainly not off researching fairies.

She'd wondered why Rock would put up with that. Except, she wouldn't. "The incident with Atti. What changed?"

Rock raised her eyebrows. Dime felt surprised, even all these cycles later, how she could read the fe'pyr like a book. A little warmth lit, and she was starting to appreciate that they really were here together. The company made her feel more confident, if she were to admit it to herself.

"We're not both here by coincidence," Dime said, trying again. "Let's just drop the walls and work together." She almost said, *like last time*, but then remembered it wouldn't be quite like last time. She avoided meeting Rock's eyes.

Rock laughed. "Direct as always. Yeah, I'm game. Friends, then. Full trust?"

"Full trust." She finally looked up, and the way Rock turned toward her, she had a feeling she'd just signed a bigger contract than she realized.

"Know Ji'Nar?" Rock started.

Dime thought. "Uh, yeah, I think so. Didn't really connect."

"Good," Rock snapped. "Ve's a crap pile. We were sent out together to see why a village was getting an increase in visitors. Sometimes it's just a good medic in town, or sometimes we have to keep an eye on one of those soft-professing holy pyrsi."

"A what?"

"You know, like a pyr that speaks in low tones and talks about peace and harmony, and manages to never pay for a meal, and soon everyone starts thinking xe's some sort of traveling messenger of Sol, even though the pyr never made any claims to be. Anyway. Not the point. In this case, I get there and figure out pretty quick there's a book in town. Written by the fairies, they say. Some farmers have it in their cottage.

"We get there and imply we're interested, but Nar starts getting super aggressive and I'm pretty sure the couple pegs him for Circles off the go. Nar doesn't realize this but goes ahead with standard procedure and casually separates them. Ve strolls outside with the ma'pyr." She made a walking gesture with her fingers.

"I'm left talking to the fe'pyr. She admits she's scared by the attention and mentions how much she doesn't want a run in with the Circles. Again, I think she suspects I'm with them, or she wouldn't be saying it. She trusts me." Rock winked at Dime. "Who wouldn't? Or maybe she's gambling on me over Nar.

"Anyway, I promise I'll look out for her. She shoves the book at me from under a seat and says please just take it. Realizing she considers this part of my promise, I do. I push it into my bag, and she relaxes a little.

"I start to ask her how she got it, but then Nar tromps in and says the ma'pyr wouldn't tell ver crap. Like, right in front of them. I imply the same. I mean, she didn't."

That's not how—

"Nar says we're wasting our time and we should all go back to Lodon, basically threatening them with a hemsa for not answering our questions. There's not even an act anymore; it's obvious ve's an agent. The ma'pyr starts to panic and the fe'pyr interrupts and says, go ahead, search the place.

"We do. I stay right with Nar. Look in every corner. Don't find anything since the book's in my bag. Ve keeps saying there's a secret compartment somewhere. I say, it's not here and we can go back now, since I don't want to spend another bell with the pyr. I tell ver maybe we got bad info.

"Ve insists on staying. Says we need to ask around the village. Later, a quick storm blows through, and what do you know, the cabin burns down."

Dime hissed.

"The couple had stepped out," Rock hurried to say. "They were safe. I mean, all their possessions destroyed and Sol knows what trauma. But physically safe.

"When Nar isn't looking, I give them what unsigned notes I had and said to get away. The fe'pyr won't look at me anymore; I think she's terrified I'll tell about the book. They're both crying. The ma'pyr's worried the fairies did it. I said, but what did the book show?

"I mean, of course I'd looked at it; it was just some storybook, not even like anything interesting. But I asked again, what did the book show? Was it wicked? The couple's too spooked; they won't even talk to me. I swore I'd help them, any way I could. Looking back, I didn't even mean them. I meant, all of it.

"I'm still not even sold on the fairies, at this point. I'm still thinking some tripped-out artist made the thing in the first place. But the charred wood of that house; *that* I'm not forgetting."

Her next words were more to herself. "Everything I'd ever believed changed that turn."

Dime wanted to say she knew how that felt, but Rock had moved on with the story.

"I confront Nar, of course. Ve acts all surprised and sad, oh the lightning struck, or oh, maybe the wicked fairies did it. Whole time ve smells like fuel." She turned right at Dime. "Ve did it. I am *certain*."

Rock paused. Dime was concerned how much the event still seemed to affect her, but seeing someone's home destroyed . . . witnessing an overt act of the Violence. Being there and not stopping it. Hard to say how that would affect a pyr. A turn ago, she had believed there was no contact with the Fo-ror, while pyrsi like Ella and Rock and, it turned out, herself were living with the scars of that myth. She—

"Got back and had a talk with Atti after the next Call to Light. Made a scene, as he put it. Because saying things you don't want to hear is always a scene, right? Anyway, I tell him his pal, Nar, committed the harmed-out straight-up Violence, and he said it would be a crime to accuse ver without proof. He aloofly whispers that the fairies did it, I mean, not even like he means it. The others couldn't hear that part, so I raised it louder.

"Basically, I'm just starting to get this creeped out feeling that we use 'the fairies' as an excuse for our own sharts, so I flip it on him and say loud enough, did you say fairies? So they're back now? Wouldn't that be a *massive issue*? I mean, I didn't see any. Maybe we oughta go just check them out and see, and maybe they can tell us nope, they weren't there; it was just Nar. Maybe the *fairies* aren't the problem here.

"I implied I knew some things, maybe even had evidence. Atti switches away from that real fast, and tells me off in front of everyone else. Said I'd twisted his words and I had three bells to decide whether I worked there anymore."

Dime had heard a bit of this story. Atti hadn't just told her off; he'd berated her in front of a whole lot of agents. Belittled her. Like he always did. Agitation gripped her. It's why she quit. But Rock hadn't quit. *Ah, Sol.* Dime looked up, eager to hear what it was she was missing.

"I decided to quit. Make my own scene of it. But someone stopped me." Rock squinted. "So, we have our trust pact, but that doesn't mean I have to reveal things that don't need to be revealed. Suffice to say, someone recruited me. Someone who actually cares about *preventing* the Violence, rather than shoveling over it."

She had an idea where this was going, but the thought stunned her. Was it Ador? The Free Winds? Would he be so bold to pluck agents? He'd always been so respectful of Dime's career and boundaries. Part of her hoped Rock wouldn't say it was Ador. Part of her hoped that she would.

"'Dawn's Circle,' they call it. Started by one of the old Lights. No, Sala doesn't know. It's run from within now. Invitation only. A shadow Circle dedicated to understanding the fairies, to be ready when the truce crumbles—or ready when pyrsi are willing to break it. Hopefully for the right reasons.

"Dime. Fairies are—"

Rock's face told it all. *She already knows. That's why she's telling me.*

They stared at each other, their expressions naked, yet neither broaching the topic. Dime tried to do it, yet her words felt locked inside. Like a prison.

Rock closed her eyes. "Your scars, of course. But it's more than that. You're different, D. Just . . . some of your sensibilities. The ones I've always— It wasn't until the fairies came to find you that I pieced it together. Dime, I know you didn't know. At least not back then. When . . . when did you find out?"

"Just turns ago. After the incident. A friend realized it. Not me." Dime resolved to keep Ella out of this for now, until she understood more about this Dawn's Circle. She was glad she didn't have to say it. The idea of being biologically Fo-ror was still formulating in her mind.

Rock, seeming to understand this, shifted back to her story. "Atti asked me directly if I had any materials related to the fairies. I could tell him I didn't. That book—I'd already given it to the others. The worst part was groveling to that turd. I apologized, said I was misguided.

"See, I didn't understand at the time the leverage I had, which is why he didn't throw me out right away. He knew what others thought of me, that my departure would open up questions. He didn't want questions. He tried to make me stay by threatening me, and he thinks he won. Since then, he lords over controlling me. Gives me horrible assignments. Thinks he's Sol.

"I don't care. I do the minimum for the report, then sneak away and do what DC needs me to do. I know who I am." Her eyes lit up. "Have you seen it? Pito?"

"No," Dime was embarrassed to admit. "I made it into some creek alley, tried to help a pyr, and got arrested."

Rock giggled. "Of course you did." A smile broke across her face.

"I did see the Crossing," Dime said.

"Oh! That place is the best. You can get some of the weirdest stuff there. And there's a hidden hall where pyrsi meet and negotiate. Do you know there's a fairy there who uses valence to remove hemsa? They say it hurts like harm, but it works."

"Really?" Dime started to think of other questions. She wanted to hear what kind of Intel Dawn's Circle—she was still adjusting to that idea—had gathered on the Fo-ror. What materials they had.

"No, not yet. I want to hear your side of it. The invasion."

Dime told the story as best she remembered it. The fairies bursting in, waving the rope. Her departure. She couldn't help but enjoy the genuine shock on Rock's face when she described falling over the cliff. She wasn't sure how appropriate it was to brag about falling over a cliff, but the story did have a certain flair.

"So you know the thing, D?" Dime was remembering now how Rock asked these completely vague questions, like you were supposed to have a witty response. She waited; Rock would answer it anyway.

"Your arrest failed because you didn't know about arrest. These fairies are so reverent about their Seats and their traditions, they'd never considered that someone wouldn't just submit."

"Then why the ropes?"

"Part show, part control. Same as these bars here. Confinement doesn't sit well with pyrsi. We're not built that way. Even if pyrsi agreed with their duty to stay, after a while, they start to justify getting out. The Seats don't want pyrsi thinking about it. Also, they needed a way to secure you in flight. Probably had a blanket to carry you in. That's why they needed three. To carry you."

Dime was going to let that last image pass for now. "So you're an expert on fairies."

"No. But I've learned a lot from the pieces DC have put together. The fairies are different from us, but a lot the same too. You know, like norside pyrsi compared to Lodon or the plains. Different culture. Different reasons to be annoyed. Still pyrsi."

She felt comforted by Rock's casual references to Dime as one of "us." To Rock, Dime was who she'd always been. Yet that wasn't all true. Nine cycles was a long time. If they were going to have any relationship now, as friends, it had to be based on who they were *now*. Except Dime was still figuring that out.

Dime reached out and ran her fingers along one of the metal bars, slightly rough, and cool to the touch. She remembered what Rock had said. Diamond dust within the metal. Imbued somehow with valence. Her fingers tingled against the cool metal, and she withdrew them.

Rock was one of the only pyrsi who knew about Dime's pendant. Dime felt grateful that, for now, Rock hadn't brought it up. Despite her bluster, Rock was always decent.

Dropping heavier topics for a while, the two caught up. On life, on assignments, on pyrsi they'd independently met. Dime relaxed into the conversation, glad to have company again. Being alone was nice some of the time. But not all.

Remembering she had her dice, she dug them out, and they played a few rounds of double-up, which was tricky since the game relied on bluffing. Rock kept glaring through the bars to make sure she could see her own rolls.

Rock threw out her hand. "*Shh.* Guard. Turn away."

Securing the dice back into her pocket, Dime turned her chair away from Rock and tried to appear grumpy.

Wayniam strode down the hall, two trays of food floating above his hands. The key flying in and out of his fingers, he opened the top sections of their doors and floated the trays in. Dime was mesmerized by the easy use of valence, though she tried not to show it to the guard.

Unsure when he'd be back for the dishes, Dime and Rock ate in silence. The food was much better than she'd expected. After a while, he came back and whisked the trays out without a word. Dime waited until his footsteps faded away.

"I don't hear anyone else here," Dime noted. It didn't seem like they'd have an empty prison set aside, just waiting for intruding Ja-lal.

"Oh, the rooms go back a ways, from what I've learned. The other pyrsi are in whole rooms, without cages. Just shaking something off or being taught a lesson. This is just a scary-looking front area, from what I can tell. Maybe it's supposed to remind you to behave when you first walk in, but it's only actually used for serious cases. Or pyrsi they haven't figured out what to do with yet, or ones the Seats want to talk to. If they decide we've committed a crime, they could move us to the back for as long as they want."

"Yeah, let's avoid that." Dime voiced the thought aloud.

"I'm glad you're safe." Rock sounded tired.

"Thanks. I am too. It was a long fall down that cliff."

"You can't keep bragging about that. It's not even competent."

"I'm not bragging!" Annoyed at her raised inflection, Dime tried to steady her voice. "So, fairy expert. I have a decision to make. I either wait here, and hope the High Seat got my hint that he'd better come find me or I'll spill their secrets. Or I let you help me break out, which I know you know how to do."

"You don't know that."

"I actually do."

"Fine. What's your goal?"

"I need to talk to the High Seat. I'm not leaving Pito until I do."

"Hmm. And you already made it into their Chambers?"

"Yes."

"Then harm that." Rock waved a hand in front of her face. "Get out of here. Show him you're in control. Go see the city so you're better informed. Or because you can. Then go back to Chambers once they're in session. Walk in, all like, hey, what's up."

Dime had been leaning the same way, but hearing Rock say it reassured her. Dime worried that her own reasons were more about being stubborn than wise, but—they couldn't *both* be wrong, right?

"Ok, so the bars are made with powdered diamonds and neither of us have valence. So, what do we do?"

"First, we *rely* on our lack of valence. Keeps their guard down. I mean, these fairies think we're animals. Not once they get to know us, but prejudices are hard to shake. So don't get fancy with them."

"I did demand to see their leader."

"I said fancy. Not bold. Know the difference. Now, only one problem."

"What's that?"

"We have to wait for Waynie to come back—and we're not staging some goofy emergency, because I have limits. Don't want him getting suspicious, anyway. After that last meal, they leave us time to sleep. So, take a nap. Chill out. Whatever. Oh, one condition."

Dime tried not to let Rock see how much it amused her that she was demanding conditions while locked in a box. Guess that was bold, not fancy. "I'm listening."

"Condition is, I stay here. I don't want them knowing we're working together, just in case things go wrong. I'd like to keep my cover for now. See, they think they caught me spying in their city. They didn't know I *wanted* to be taken here. Now that you're safe, I'll stick around and learn what else I can."

Rock rubbed her hand a little. "It's like I heal faster here." She glanced at Dime. "Oh, nothing to worry about; I was just messing with the lock and cut my hand. Do not challenge a diamond, by the way; the diamond will win."

"That's what I've always said!" Dime followed it with a little whistle.

"Stop that."

Rock spent a few strides searching through her pockets. Dime rolled her own sleeves up, looking at her cuts. They didn't seem much different. She rolled them back down.

"Hey," Rock said.

"Hey, what?"

"The promise holds. Whatever happens in all this . . . same team?"

"Sure, Rock."

Rock twirled something small in her hands. Dime watched her, not remembering her ever this uneasy. Whatever age granted in confidence, it did tend to exact payment in assuredness.

"We'll work together. I promise."

"*Pssst.* Sleepy."

"*Hrmm?*"

"He'll be back before too long. I need to give you something."

Dime didn't realize she'd fallen asleep, but as her eyes opened, she saw metal bars, striping her view of the ceiling above, and felt the bed beneath her. Thin, but comfortable.

"Come on, sit up. We should have done this by now, but I didn't want to wake you."

Grumbling, Dime pulled herself to a seat. She'd even kicked her boots off; she found them and slid each back on.

Rock was holding onto the bars, something grasped in her fingers. "I need to throw this to you. Now—and this is important—you *have* to catch it. If it falls out on the floor we're in big trouble." Rock pointed to the space between the cages.

Dime waved her hand. "Don't put that on me. Can you tie a string to it? I know you have a string."

Rock grimaced, but a moment later she'd tied a string to what looked like a long, narrow key. "Ready?"

Dime nodded. Rock deftly threw the little key through the bars, where Dime missed it and it clattered to the floor.

"Careful! Don't break the glass!"

Glass? As Dime untied the string, she noticed there was a crystal lodged in the key's top. "Key swap?"

"Don't overcomplicate if you don't need to." Rock grinned as she whisked the string back into her own cage, wrapping it back around her fingers before pushing it into a pocket. "Do I need to explain this?"

"No, I get it. Sol, Rock, he'll really have to not be paying attention."

"It's fine. They're used to watching for valence. He won't expect this. He's looking for fancy."

"Not bold." Dime couldn't hold back a grin.

She lodged the key into her sleeve, before taking a trip back to her commode.

"They make Wayniam clean those too," Rock called. "Dead caves are too sensitive for their cleaning crew. Like our dens. It's quite the assignment."

Ella had mentioned the dead caves several times. Dime glanced around the blackened rock walls. More stories here, she supposed.

It was at least another bell until the guard came meandering down the passage with two more trays of food hovering over his hands. He looked most annoyed to see the two fe'pyrsi in their cages, ironically, since surely he expected them to be there. Dime remembered to act like she was paying Rock no attention.

"Hey, Wayn!" Rock called. He glared in her direction, almost with a hiss. His key flew into Rock's cage door, and the top panel swung open. Wayniam guided one tray of food through the opening, landing it on her table. He closed the panel, and the key flew back into his grasp.

He walked over to Dime's cage. "You? Nothing to say?"

Dime was looking down at the floor, a hand on her back. "Guard Wayniam, it feels like there's a lump in this mattress. Could I get a new one?"

Wayniam guided Dime's meal tray onto a wood table not far from her cage. An extraordinarily old-looking one too; Dime had been curious how long it had been there.

"Sit in the chair," he commanded. "And promise me you won't get up."

"I promise," Dime reassured him, moving the chair away from the bed toward the front side of the cage and plopping down into it, sitting on her hands. "Look, right there. I didn't want to get in trouble for messing with the bed, not when I'm waiting here for the High Seat."

Wayniam shook his head with deliberate incredulity. "You're really serious about that? Keep waiting. Now, where?"

Dime pointed to the foot of the bed, then sat back on her hands.

The key flew from Wayniam's hand and into the lock, clicking. Keeping an eye on Dime, he swung the door open, again without touching it, and walked in. Reaching the mattress and pressing his hands on it, Wayniam grunted. "Well. There's just something in there. Give me a flap."

During the time Wayniam stuck himself half under the slightly levitating mattress, Dime reached over and switched out the key, shoving her hands back under her seat as Wayniam wriggled back out. His wings popped up behind him and he waved a small bag at her. "This was jammed in the slats." He pulled open the drawstring and looked inside. "It's a bag of nuts. Stashed away, I suppose. They still look good," he added, clipping them to his belt.

Dime scooted, still in the chair, back to the table, moving herself further away from the door. She angled the table in front of her as Wayniam waved the food tray into her cell and sat it down in front of her, a variety of food items jostling slightly as the tray clattered into place. Dime reached for a chunk of soft bread, tearing off a smaller piece. "Thank you," she said. "Looks wonderful."

With a begrudging nod, Wayniam stepped back into the corridor. Rock's key flew into his hands. In a moment of panic, Dime heard the door slam shut, but without the usual *click*. Without giving Wayniam time to consider it, she bounded from the chair and threw her fingers around the bars, one hand on the door and the other on its frame, ignoring the tingling that ran through her hands at the valence-charged cage.

"Please, Guard Wayniam, tell the High Seat that I need to talk to him. It's important." She pretended to shake the bars, as if trying to open the door.

"Ugh. Brutes." Wayniam hurried back down the passage without another look.

"Is he really going to eat those nuts?" Dime asked. They were perfectly fine and seasoned with Ella's own spice rub. Still, Dime wasn't sure she'd eat anything of indeterminate age found under a bed.

"He will," Rock said. "Without doubt."

"I don't like messing with him," Dime said with a sigh. "Feels dishonest."

"He locked you in a cage."

"Doesn't impact my choices."

Rock groaned. "You were an agent for cycles, D. You supported this very sort of thing. Innocent pretense, in the name of peace. This is different?"

"Well, I stopped." Dime had done good, also. It was all, just, getting confusing.

"The Circles want everything to be perfect. Life isn't perfect. The world isn't perfect. It's our choices that matter. What we're willing to do and why. It's taken me a long time to learn that, so don't laugh at it. Hey. There's more at stake here than Guard Wayniam. He's not even that nice. It's not like you knocked him over; you just stole his key."

STOLE. Dime looked at the key in her hand.

"Stop it! Go give it back, then. Or leave it there. Anyway, go find the High Seat. Before Grumpy Guard comes back for the dishes."

Turning the key in her fingers, Dime set it on the table. There was no way she was leaving a hunk of warm bread to cool. Dipping it into a little dish of spicy oil, she chomped the doughy bread down. Seeing a few other items that would keep, she nestled them in her bag, folding the serving paper around them as best she could.

Not knowing what to say to Rock, and certain that, this time, they'd cross paths again, she gave the fe'pyr a curt nod and disappeared down the hall, the cage door clanging shut behind her.

Dime wasn't ready to be seen. With the patience of a master realms player using xyr spy, she crept down each passage. Hiding when needed, she slipped through dark corridors, avoiding those whose stones looked recently lit.

She presumed that valence charged the glowing stones. It seemed that pyrsi could relight them, and over time they would fade. Anger rose in her, thinking what life would be like here without wings. Flying wasn't everything; there must be ways to climb. But even the lights depended on valence, which depended on wings. Wings she'd been born with.

Even the chandelier lights in Chambers had dimmed by the time she reached the large hall. A lone pyr swept the floor, but with a broom like a Ja-lal would, not with valence. The fairy's wings were folded behind xem, swooshing in opposition as xe swept.

Trying to imitate the accent Wayniam had used, Dime called around a bend. "Hi, there. I'm new with the guards and thought Wayniam would be here. When do they start up again?"

"Wayniam?" Xe was trying to sound polite, Dime could tell, like xe might be talking to someone of higher rank. "He's not here; he works in the dead caves. Chambers convene at first light, like always. But you need to report to the caves. No one allowed here."

"Oh, was confused." Knowing her accent must be off, she tried to muddle it. "They were meeting here earlier."

"Sure, some sort of emergency. Got called in myself." Dime could hear the unspoken reproof, *Go to the caves like I told you and let me finish.*

Before she provoked suspicion, Dime slipped away again. Waiting for a while in a corridor, she saw a pyr, maybe another of the cleaners, trudging down a hall with xyr hair tied into a cloth and a bag over one arm. At a distance, Dime followed. Finally reaching what appeared to be an exit, the pyr barely stopped, walking on through and flying up into the sky just steps from the doorway.

Dime peered around the edge. A guard was staring off into the distance, so Dime walked on through. Though, she figured, if xe was there to verify who could get in, it wouldn't be so easy on the way back. She'd deal with that later.

As soon as she was outside, she turned a hard right and paused behind a tree. If xe'd heard her, xe'd just figure she'd flown off. A few minutes later, Dime wandered out again, walking briskly from the complex.

She didn't take the cloak out of her bag. She'd never litter it, but she agreed with Rock; her instinct against the things had been right after all, whatever Ella said. But it wasn't because of the Circles' rules. This was who Dime was. And she wasn't going to hide. That said, she meant to avoid any further contact with marshals, for the time being.

Taking off her bag, she sat back near a wide trunk and watched the fairies flying above. As they flitted between wood-planked walkways surrounding what she could make out as larger structures, she again considered how much she stood out here without wings. How difficult getting around would be, the way things were built. She looked for ladders or ramps, but didn't see any.

Through the trees, a clearing caught her eye. It looked intentional, or maybe the spot of an old fire. Walking toward it, she saw ch'pyrsi zipping back and forth in the air, tossing a bright yellow ball around. Sometimes if the ball didn't take the right path, it would switch course in midair. And if it was dropped, it would curve around, returning to waiting arms.

Listening to the laughs and shouts of the young fairies, their wings flapping behind them, she had a suspicion they weren't supposed to be practicing valence on their own. Dime grinned, remembering how strictly she'd been told not to play near the ravines.

The playing ch'pyrsi restored a positive feeling in her. One she'd lost but now knew she needed. Her interactions with the Fo-ror had not been positive, so far, yet she knew she couldn't judge a whole culture on touchpoints of long-standing, cultivated tension. And so the ch'pyrsi brought her hope.

Dime thought about these innocent pyrsi, probably being taught the same awful things about her she'd been taught about them. She wished she could tell them. Tell their parents. Tell everyone. What she could do for now was foster change. She wasn't quite sure how, yet, but she would figure it out.

Reaching into her backpack, she took out the rest of her prison meal, at least what hadn't been too messy to pack. A rolled sandwich, made of thin bread, a sliced dein, some sprouts, and a creamy green spread, had been neatly cut into halves, then wrapped tightly into paper. She took her time eating it, enjoying each bite.

A mix of crunchy yellow kernels had been tucked into a serving paper. Dime unfolded it, enjoying the pop of each in her mouth. She took a stick and poked the used wrappings down into the ground, where they'd dissolve and return to the soil.

From her flask, she drank down a measure of water. She'd need to find more of that soon. Glancing at the bottle, she had the wild idea to just ask.

She strolled down a worn dirt pathway until she saw a pyr tending to a flower bed underneath a tree. Red blooms were each given space to grow, in front of a ring of wildflowers. A long bench sat beside it, facing the garden on one side and the path on the other.

A little hanging windchime reminded her of Ella's tower. Ella loved chimes and bells, and Dime loved them too—ok, except the sharp-toned one Ella kept in her pocket and used to call Dime in for meals. She imagined Suzanne'd had thoughts on that one too. But here, under the massive tree, the chimes tinkled in harmony with the breeze.

Dime was always drawn to gardeners; to put so much love into caring for another spoke to one's pyrsonality. So she took the risk. "Hello," Dime said. "Please don't be scared. I'm a Ja-lal. My name's Fe'Dime."

The pyr froze, so Dime hurried over her words. "I won't tell anyone I was here. I'd like to refill my water." She held up her flask. "Is there a common well? I could tell you my story, but I think it might be better just to say I mean no harm."

The pyr hadn't moved. Dime worried at xyr response.

"If you want me to leave, I understand. My pyrsi, we've been taught the same about you. I'm learning none of it is true. I'm sorry to shock you this way. I suppose I've had a lot of shocks myself lately."

Not sure what else to say, Dime waited as the pyr tried to grasp Dime's words. She hoped she hadn't frightened xem too much.

"Is this a prank?" xe asked.

Dime turned around and lowered her backpack, showing her finely stitched tunic with no possibility of wings underneath it. As she put her pack on again, she said, "I'm sorry. Maybe this was too much. I'm learning to handle things myself and I'm tired of hiding."

The pyr paused. "That we have in common. Here. What flask do you have?" Dime handed her flask to the pyr. Xe flew upward with it, returning a couple of strides later to hand her the flask, now full. Xe appeared less stunned, but still tense.

"I'll go now. But, if you don't mind, how many bells until dawn?"

"Bells?" The pyr scrunched xyr face.

Ella had indicated that they used the same measures of time. But, now that Dime thought about it, she hadn't heard bells here.

"You really are from up there," the pyr said, speaking slowly, peering at Dime as if trying to find something. "Perhaps you mean spans? It should be about two more spans, by the charge in my stones." A soft glow emanated from above, where the pyr had flown for water.

"Yes, thank you," Dime said. She wasn't entirely sure bells and spans were the same, but with so much else in common, she had a sense they were similar.

"You're welcome. If you won't tell anyone you were here, I'm Ma'Rilario."

"I won't say a word. And your flowers, they're beautiful."

Rilario broke into a small smile, and Dime continued down the path, wondering if he'd believe his own memory when light dawned. Dime remembered looking into the eyes of a fairy for the first time, and knew, then, that he would.

Dime thought about Rock as she walked through the dark forest night. She'd never even considered running into another agent here, let alone someone she'd dated.

Thinking about it, they'd never formally separated. Being field agents, it'd just seemed it wouldn't be long until their next assignment together. But Dime had been sent surwes, and soon after, she'd been taken off of field duty altogether. Rock had been sent sureas, and continued on with that line of work. They hadn't seen each other again.

Dime had kept up with the agent's success over the cycles, not so much intentionally, but always with an ear of interest when her name came up. Always praised for her skill, her reports, and her dedication, Rock had been mentioned here and there. Dime had never known how to communicate her admiration to the fe'pyr. She'd held it inside, for when they met again. Instead, she'd met Dayn—they'd fallen in love, they'd been given the opportunity for children not once, but twice, and her life had moved on.

Her Circlemates hadn't known about her relationship with

Rock; it hadn't lasted that long, in truth. But Dime had treasured it.

Now, Dime had been in trouble and the agent had rushed to her rescue. For Dawn's Circle? Or for Dime?

Within takes of meeting again, they'd sealed some sort of pact. Or something. It had happened quickly. Maybe Dime was too trusting. With Juni. With Ella. With Rock. But truth was, Dime's friends always seemed to drift away over time, so the few that stayed close to her were more precious than anything. And seeing Rock again had been . . . unexpected. Nice.

If Dime's downfall was trusting a friend, she'd accept that outcome.

Yet now, Rock stayed back in the prison. Wayniam would know that he'd been tricked. Rock could talk her way out of knowing anything about it; harm, she'd probably called for the guard herself once Dime had enough time to get out. Dime resolved to try and check back with her before she left again; maybe then she'd be ready to go.

Dime thought again about her family. She and Dayn had each been accustomed to taking solo trips away, but she'd never gone so long without seeing her loved ones. Though they were always in her mind, she'd focused on herself these last turns, just trying to deal with the unknown so she could get back to them soon. Here, strolling underneath Pito, she *missed* them.

And it was more than being away from them. It was the circumstance—leaving without closure. Relying on Ella's assurance that they were safe. That Dayn had received Dime's note and understood it.

She hoped they weren't worrying about her too much.

The plan solidified in her mind. At the light of day, she would find Ferala and she would speak to him. Then, once she checked to see if Rock needed help getting out, she would return to Lodon, danger or not, and she would see her family again.

Gazing up, Dime envied the view the fairies must have in their homes above her. She wondered if they could see the skystones through the trees, not just the soft beams of filtered light that echoed down to the lower levels of the forest.

A pyr flew overhead and Dime was feeling bold.

"Burge? Excuse me?" The fairy hovered, as if waiting for Dime to catch up. When she did not, xe lowered xemself to the forest path.

"Please don't be scared," Dime repeated. "I am Fe'Dime, a Ja-lal. I mean no harm. I'm here to see someone, but I haven't found them yet. I'll go home once I do. If you'd like to leave now, I understand."

"What'd you stop me for?"

Xyr lack of reaction seemed odd; maybe xe still didn't believe her. "Oh, I wanted to know if there was a way to climb up there, just so I could see the city. Surely some residents can't fly or fly easily? And the elderly?"

"Of course," xe said. "But they usually just stay up there." Xe made an exaggerated gesture.

"That's terrible," Dime couldn't stop herself from saying. "Why don't you just build ramps?"

"Some do. But then how would you get to the next place? It's easier just to call in a lift. I do it all the time. I mean, lift, not get lifted." He hiccupped, stumbling back. Dime looked at him with suspicion.

The pyr started to fly away, but stopped and turned back. "I've had a couple of drinks," xe said, "and I'm trying to figure if this is real."

"It's real for now. Maybe a dream later." If xe'd been drinking, Dime wasn't going to bother him. She started to walk away.

"Hey, you got any snacks?"

Dime turned back around, finding the question oddly uniting. "Uh, sure." She reached into a side pocket and took out a stick. "Spicy dried fruit? It's a Ja-lal specialty. Hot peppers and fruit, rolled into sticks and dried. My favorite. Here, have one." Probably better for xem to eat a little anyway.

"Whoa, I'm not trying to *take* from you. But, like, you wanna see up there? I could give you a lift. And you could give me that." He pointed at Dime's hand. "Come on, it'll be fun. I was going there anyway."

"You can't *lift* me," Dime said, laughing. "And, Burge, are you sure you're alright?" Dime was starting to doubt that it had only been a couple of drinks.

"Sure, I can lift you. I'm a lifter. I'm no Burge!" Xe laughed. "I'm Ma'Deberele. Dime, right?"

"Here, just take the snack," she waved out the stick. Deberele looked mortally offended.

Maybe it was her endless journeys, or her constant turning around, but Dime had a moment of feeling reckless. And she didn't want the pyr to be offended over a fruit stick. "Ok, fine." She leaned her backpack behind a tree and handed him the snack, which he stuck in a pocket. So, he was serious about lifting her, then. "Just . . . *try* it first. Just a little. Don't go too high."

The pyr reached his arms under Dime's armpits and, without warning, they flew into the air. Dime threw her arms around his neck, squealing. Instead of hovering, he yelled, "See!" and continued to rise up into the air, weaving through the branches. Elated by the rush of wind past her and the sensation of rising high into the trees, Dime resolved *not* to look down, and *not* to let go.

As they broke above the level of the walkways, Dime saw more of the glowing stones, illuminating rings of boardwalks, sometimes separate, sometimes crossing. Inside each were wooden structures topped with coverings of branches and twigs. The roofs overlapped the structures, sometimes even much of the walkway. For rain more than light, she supposed.

The top level of the canopy wove above them. Through the gaps, she could see the dots of the skystones, their light shining down through the trees, forming shifting shapes on the wooden planks. In the distance, fairies flew between layers of walkways and structures, conducting their business amidst the calm of night.

She couldn't see inside any of the buildings, but even from here, they made an artful landscape—skyscape?—that she wouldn't have imagined just from the idea of an elevated structure. Pointed roofs and draping cloths, dotting through the leaves, the wooden walkways swept around with the flair of an artist's brush.

Taken by the scenery, Dime almost forgot she'd entrusted her life into the unsteady arms of a drunken fairy. They hovered for a long moment, then Deberele swooped down again, toward a small structure. Unsure if he was growing tired, Dime hesitated to stop him. He set her down on a rough floormat of woven branches and offered her his hand.

Glad he'd landed safely and, figuring now that she was here, she might as well see a real fairy's home, Dime took his outstretched hand. "Through here," he said, stepping in through a curtain, which he pushed to the side. Apparently, the curtain was the entrance, as there were no solid doors. They stepped through together, Dime watching her feet to make sure there wasn't a step down.

A tall pyr with a dark green robe and a bright orange cloth around her hair came stomping toward them as Dime looked back up, switching xyr gaze back and forth between Deberele's sweet smile and Dime's facial tattoos. "I knew it. I told you to get out, but you can't— Who the kill is this? Holy Sha!" The fairy jumped back. "Are you serious?"

"Sweetie, you said I could come back. I'm here to apologize." Deberele hiccupped, loudly this time. "Fe'Dime, this is Fe'Yaliea. Sweetie, wanna meet Dime? She's a real brute! We—"

"Whoa!" Dime interrupted. "Ok, first, I'm a Ja-lal. Long story. I wanted to see Pito, and I ran into Deberele, who flew me up here. I figured we were going to *his* home. And for nothing pyrsonal! I just wanted to see for a moment how fairies live. I'm so sorry; I would never intrude! I'm so sorry." Dime whisked her hands over her heart.

The pyr started to laugh, speaking in agitated yet sing-song voice. "Dime? Yes, that's exactly what would happen in my life. An alien species invades the Heartland and takes *one flap* to figure out that my *ex is a piece of garbage*. Good job, 'Dime.'"

She turned to Deberele. "Hairless fe'pyrsi? That's what you're up to these turns? *Gross.* Now you get out of here and wipe that gunk off her face and don't come back. It will take a whole lot more than *a fake alien* with a *terrible accent* to win me back, Deberele. When I said *impress me,* I meant by getting your *crap* together."

Dime allowed herself one quick—very quick—glance around the space. The construction relied heavily on wood and reeds, but with its variety of angles, there was a natural flow to it, like homes were meant to grow in trees. Wide beams, cushioned benches with curved seats, a small stove raised on a stone base. The smell of herbs. Lovely knotwork on the walls. A circular table with papers spread over it. She wished she could absorb it more.

But she was feeling the same about Deberele that Yaliea was.

"Come on, *Sweetie,*" Dime said. "It didn't work." Backing out of the room and awkwardly stepping up backward through the curtain, for apparently the pyr hadn't looked for her wings, she gasped as the wind almost blew her from the walkway. She clung to the side of the cottage—treehouse?—and pressed her face against the boards. "Deberele," she bellowed. "You fly me down immediately."

Without question, the pyr grabbed her again and soon they were back on the ground, Dime collapsing to her hands and knees in relief. "Go. Eat that jerky. Get home and sleep it off. And when you wake up . . . just, leave Yaliea alone. It's not going to work; trust me."

Stumbling, Deberele launched himself into the air and flew away on a jagged course.

Dime decided she'd interacted enough for the night. She'd given up on finding one of those ramps, anyway. Now that she saw how high she'd have to climb, she knew she'd be too exposed. And it was a long way down if she was seen. Already horrified that she'd let him take her so high, she decided this was one story she'd keep to herself.

After retrieving and strapping on her backpack, Dime stayed in the shadows, finally reaching a low hill with a small view of the sky. Finishing the water in her flask, she sat onto a soft patch of three-leaf, leaning back against her bag. The night spread before her: a canvas of layered textures illuminated by the glow of stones, both in the sky above and woven into the trees. Like a whole world made of glitter.

Tum would like that. She wished Tum were here.

Dime sang to herself, letting herself sink into the peace of the evening and thinking about her children. Her spouse. How Rock had actually traveled here, looking for her.

Rock had stayed on Dime's mind these last bells. She wasn't sure how to piece the pyr back into her life again. Rock had been a trailing whisper. A frayed ribbon. Dime had felt sadness over the cycles at that missing ending, she now realized. But maybe there was a way to reconnect.

She was feeling rested and at peace as Sol's light slowly crept through the boughs above. She wasn't as worried about being seen as she'd thought, even in the light. It was clear the pyrsi here stayed up top, with the exception of gardens and parks—and the government complex, which protruded from the ground, she supposed because of the caves.

Besides, even if someone spotted her and cared, they'd just take her back to the complex. She still had one card she hadn't played. One big card. And she felt certain that Ferala knew. This time, she knew how to approach him. She thought she understood.

The light was burgeoning as Dime walked back to the edge of the complex, locating the arched doorway set against a rocky wall. The guard sat near the entrance, clutching a book. As pyrsi arrived for work, the guard would look them over as they passed by.

She thought about just walking up and demanding an audience, but there had been politics at play in Chambers. Until she could talk to the High Seat, she didn't want to take a chance of being diverted— or locked up without a way out this time. And she felt sure that, this time, she needed to get to him in private.

Reaching into her pack, she tied a climbing hook to a thin rope. Staying patient, she waited until there was no one in sight.

With a grunt, she hurled it up into the tree. To her dismay, it rattled around, making a clattering of leaves and clamor before thumping down into the dirt. Crouching low, she held her breath.

The guard stood, staring up into the tree. "*Hmm,*" he grumbled. Sitting down again, he scanned up and down, his eyes searching the surrounding sky as Dime crouched, hidden, in the brush. Knowing she had to make it just a little farther, she heaved the hook as best she could and hoped Sol was on her side.

The metal hooked over a branch and Dime shook it several times, yanking down on the rope to cause as much commotion as possible. Not even looking at the ground, the guard flew up into the leaves. "Hey! Who's there!"

Dime darted through the passage.

Remembering the turns as best she could, she did not run for Chambers, but into the warren of passages behind the big hall. She stopped at voices, waiting in shadows and behind doors, taking one turn at a time, until she saw what she sought: a diamond-pinned guard.

To her shock, she saw xe was one of the pyrsi who had invaded her home in the first place. Strolling down the passage, xe appeared to be sipping some brew.

Dime popped in front of xem, watching xyr eyes widen. Dime's own trepidation calmed at the pyr's shock, the scenario reversed. Xe was just a pyr, after all. "Will we always meet under such unexpected circumstances?" Feeling the peace of Sol's rising light in her heart, she smiled. "I'm Fe'Dime. I'm here to see the High Seat."

"You should have come the first time," xe whispered, beckoning her to follow.

"Then, Burge, you should have asked."

Dime couldn't see xyr reaction as, with a wave, the guard dimmed the lights around them, ignoring the shouts and calls as pyrsi struggled to relight the stones in their wake. The guard led the way around several bends, and then xe stopped midway through a hall, Dime almost running into xem in the darkness. Dime heard a rustling against the wall, like a tapestry moving, and then a panel swung open.

As they stepped through and the door closed behind them, Dime blinked at the return of light. A soft light, through curved forms of glass that covered the glowing stones. The corridor was covered in fine, dark woods and deeply carved trim. Doors lined one side of the hall, the other had only a set of double doors, with one cracked open to reveal an extravagantly appointed lounge beyond.

At the end of the corridor, the guard halted her, peering around the corner. "Hurry," xe said, and Dime followed xem across an empty room, which opened into three large corridors. Again peering down one first, the guard led her toward the door at the end of the hall.

The office beyond was richly decorated, full of artifacts and detailed statues. It was empty. "Go inside," xe snapped.

Dime paused. The room did not remind her of the stylings of Ferala. "Is this the High Seat's office?" She stepped away, so that xe'd truly have to force her inside if xe chose to do so.

"Please, I urge you. We must not attract attention."

Dime did not believe xyr polite change in tone, and stood in place.

Xyr tone intensified. "You must have your audience in private or you'll be sent back to the cells." Xe leaned in. "We've increased the security. Substantially."

She worried what that meant for Rock. Yet Dime, looking at the guard's same cold frown as when xe'd invaded her home, could not think about Rock right now. Rock could handle herself. She brushed her worry aside.

"Please, visitor. *Go in*."

Footsteps interrupted them, and Dime saw a figure down the hallway, exiting another office with a stack of papers. This was not a Seat. Xe stopped. "Hello," Dime waved, making sure to be seen.

The pyr shuffled toward them, and Dime noted xyr nervous grimace. The guard pasted on a fake smile.

"She's with me, Tikinal," the guard clipped, as much as the smooth fairy pronunciation could be clipped. "Get *in*," xe said to Dime.

Now what did I tell you?

"Honorous Tikinal," Dime said, staying right where she stood. "It looks like the High Seat is not in his chamber. Can you ensure he is aware of my arrival?"

"Honorous?" the guard mocked. "He's a clerk. Tikinal, I am under orders. Move along."

Dime and Tikinal locked eyes.

"Seat Neimano is not in his study." His voice was almost steady, but Dime detected a slight quiver. "I believe he left for Chambers."

He tore his gaze away from Dime, forcing himself to look at the guard. He smiled. "I will escort her to the High Seat, who is in. Come, this way."

Tikinal walked down the corridor and Dime followed. For a moment, Dime thought the guard would try and stop them. Instead, xe turned and left. Dime looked at the clerk.

His robes were simple, and of course his face was unmarked. His hair, not that she meant to be superficial, stunned her. Shades of white and gray, appearing to be natural, wove in and out of a large bundle, pinned to the top of his head with what reminded her of decorative climbing spikes. If climbing spikes were decorative.

"Thank you," Dime whispered. "Whatever you hear, I am no one's enemy."

"I'm afraid, visitor, that I now am." He nodded. "May your meeting be productive."

Tikinal escorted her down the center corridor, to the door in the back. "You will only get one chance," he whispered, peeking in through a crack in the door. "Go."

Dime walked inside, and the door shut behind her.

There, in a fine study lined with books and centered by a chandelier of brightly glowing stones, a pyr stood up from behind a desk. As he walked to meet her, his dark gray face bore no expression. His floor-length white braids were accented with silver threads, the braids woven again into groups, one hanging at each side. Shining, iridescent wings rose behind him, highlighting the blue and silver embroidery of his layered gown. He clasped his hands together, his fingers covered in diamond rings.

"Ma'Ferala," he introduced himself. "I suppose we should talk."

Interlude

His name had become much grander for all the food he'd brought back to the troop. He felt proud, but not happy. Love was not well.

She had a good name too, almost as good as his, but he liked to think of her as Love, because that was how he felt thinking about her.

Love was sick.

Her tummy hurt from the strong Sha water. She spent most of the time in her burrow now, saying things he didn't want to remember. He wanted to bring her softer water, but no matter how many ways he tried to carry it back from the forest's edge, it slipped through his hands.

Instead, he brought her plump fruits. They had a little water in them, even if it was mixed with fruit.

He growled at the rope net in front of him, tugging at it as hard as he could. He knew not to bite it. The rope was wicked and it had damaged his teeth. Now he had bad teeth and the net was still there.

Seeing a puddle, he lapped water from it. It was almost good water, and he felt sad drinking it when Love could not have any.

He missed Home Sha. He wanted to go back there. He was old enough to remember it; some of the cubs had never lived there. That was bad. If he could know when something was bad, he did not know why the flying two-legs could not know.

Maybe they were not as smart.

Or maybe they did not care when others were sad.

Thinking of something very funny, he pulled back his lips and screeched, pounding his fists onto the floor. Maybe it was not right to laugh when Love was sick. Or maybe he would tell Love and she would laugh too.

Either way, he was going to do it.

He moved up next to the net, squatted down, and made a big poop. He pooped right next to the net. Think about this! Those flying two-legs would come to check their net that keeps the troop away. And they would smell his poop.

That was a funny thing!

He moved away and rubbed his bottom all along the grass, taking care not to dirty or ruffle his feathers. Then he went back to look at his poop.

It was a huge poop. It was soft and piled like a tiny mountain. And it smelled so bad!

Hmm. Maybe this was bad. Maybe Boss would say you know better than to do bad. Bad is forbidden. Someone else doing a bad does not make your bad good.

Now he was worried. He did not want to lose some of his name for doing a bad thing. Glancing a moment at the big poop, he did not scrape it away. Maybe Sha would grant him one bad thing.

Moving down the net, he stood as tall as he could to try and pick the fruits that were still on trees. These were the best fruits; they were not mushy.

Carrying all that he could fit in his arms, he ran back toward their Beds. And he decided he would not tell Love the funny thing after all. Maybe she would tell Boss. He would just try and not do a bad thing again.

He did hope Love would like the fruit and maybe be a little less sad.

Act 3

ADAMANTINE

"I'm Fe'Diamond. And I'm too angry to worry over whether I'm doing this right, so here goes. I understand you're the leader of the Fo-ror. I understand there are protocols I should follow in your presence. However, for reasons of which you are likely aware, I've never been taught those protocols.

"Instead, my house was invaded and my family disrupted. My city was thrown into disarray. I've endured extended pain and hunger. I almost died. I've been locked in a cage. And those seem to be the least of any concerns, from the impression I'm getting around here. So, it's just us. I'd appreciate if we could speak freely and frankly."

Ferala's face remained drawn. "Could I provide anything for you? Some tea?"

Dime took a breath. "No, thank you. High Seat, why did you arrest me?"

"Please, will you sit?" He waved his arm, and a large cushioned stool floated toward her. Dime set her backpack to the side, stepped in front of the stool, and sat back.

"Why did you arrest me?"

Ferala walked behind his own desk, sitting into his chair as his wings spread to the sides. "If our words are truly private . . . I did not issue your arrest."

"But the—" Dime almost snapped back, but then she remembered the diamond-pinned guard was not planning on taking her here. Dime nodded, certain shadows now forming into shapes.

"I am unfond of secrets," she said.

"Burgess Diamond, I have lived my life amongst secrets."

"By your choice, if you're in charge." Dime raced through the questions in her mind, tiring of this banter. She hadn't traveled across Ada-ji for banter.

He sat back further. "You oversimplify, as all who glare upward will do. For the Fo-ror, no pyr is in charge, no matter their status. Tradition rules us. As it should. The way of Sha." He made a curved-handed gesture with which Dime was not familiar. "That is greater than any pyr."

This struck her less as something the Circles would say, and more like Sol's Pillars. Justifying everything without providing a justification. Even without the Pillars' vicious tone, the similarity disturbed her. He drew his tea closer, the polished stoneware floating to meet his hand.

"Valence is used so commonly. For minutia," she muttered, while trying to think how to ask again about the arrest.

"Valence is dangerous," he responded, tipping the cup and saucer to his lips. Wincing, he glanced toward the closed door and then pushed the cup to the side. "A burden."

"Not too dangerous for common tasks. For convenience."

"These uses, they are trivial. Using a hand to grasp a cup is not like using a hand to strike a foe. The greater power a pyr executes, the greater danger they risk."

"Show me."

Ferala sat straighter in his chair. "Show you?"

"Yes, show me your valence. Impress me with the power of the Fo-ror, so I know to return home. To never interrupt or disturb you again." Dime didn't know why she was taunting him, but a temper was rising in her. Maybe she wanted to test whether he'd insult her the way Dailawe had. Or maybe because his ch'pyrish explanations were insulting her already.

"You have no idea what you are saying." Ferala's face bore no expression, but his eyes signaled alarm.

"You're correct. I know so little. Now, why is that?" Dime paused. "I told you, I'm not here to exchange pleasantries, High Seat. I mean you no disrespect; I just want answers to my questions. I believe I deserve them."

"Tell me," Ferala said, as if he hadn't heard her, "tell me about Sol's Reach." Dime noted that he had called the northern lands by their Ja-lal name, not the Barrens as they were commonly called here in the forest.

"It is my home," Dime answered honestly. "It has diverse landscapes, ranging from flat plains to rocky hills and towering mountains. The city of Lodon rests like a rough-hewn jewel set among them, its towers rising to reach Sol. In day, the light gleams from the golden peaks of the highest towers. At night, the reflection of the skystones filters through the lattices and windows and creates corridors of soft light to complement the corridors of stone."

She glanced around the small room, devoid of windows yet elegant with its books and carvings and small works of art. "I miss my home."

Ferala started to respond then stopped, as if realizing she did not mean the lands of the Fo-ror. "I have never ventured there," he said instead. "I have had no reason. It is said to be terrible. Dry, barren. Ruthless."

"It is not," Dime said. She felt no need to defend her home to a pyr who had never bothered to understand it. Yet, for his potential to influence others, she could not let the ignorance pass. "Describing the greatness of Sol's Reach would require more time than we have. Its stalwart ethic, its vibrant celebrations, its compassion. The caring and resources offered freely to all pyrsi." She considered, a moment, what she thought of when she thought of home. "Tell me, High Seat, are you close to anyone?"

"I have a spouse. Of many cycles." Ferala's demeanor shifted, unable to hide the look of a pyr still in love after a lifetime. To that, Dime felt a stride of connection.

"I have a spouse also. A Ja-lal. He is warm, kind, and funny. Seeing him, to me, is like meeting the rising of Sol: warmth upon my face and clarity in my sight. I have two children. Also Ja-lal. They are good pyrsi. Precious to me and to anyone who knows them." She waited, hoping he would see the emotion in her eyes also. "There will never be true peace between us if you dismiss us as unworthy. As unequal."

Ferala lifted his gaze, but would not meet hers. "It is clear to me that the long-held state of withdrawn relations between our societies is tenuous. For cycles, we have tried to stay this flood, but its walls are crumbling. I do not see such events leading to peace. Only more War. If you value peace, you should leave and never return. Or is there something else you want?"

Dime had used the word *peace* in its general context, but hadn't considered it in the context of truly returning . . . *War*. Did Ferala consider this lack of overt conflict to be peace? Dime did not. And what did she want? She'd been focused on getting answers about herself and what had transpired in Lodon, but what was her goal? To return things to their previous state? To go back to pretending the other didn't exist? She didn't know if that was possible, especially now for her.

And here this leader was, expecting her to have a plan or perhaps items for negotiation, while all she'd been focused on was understanding her own past. She felt smaller for it. But, why was any of this relying on her in the first place? She wasn't the leader of a society; he was. Her temper grew; it was the same with the Circles. Always pointing fingers, when they held the power. "I'll be honest with you. I don't know what I want anymore. Control was ripped out of my hands when your guards disrupted my family, and now you're staring back at me, like what do *I* want?"

Ferala shifted, just slightly.

"You know, I want you to answer my questions, which is why I endured a long journey, a dangerous climb, and being put into a *box* to get here."

Clarity surged in her mind, sharpened by her anger. Dime had risked her safety and her ability to return to her family, yet she had still learned nothing. She was not his advisor, nor was she his travel guide. At any moment, this pyr could have her dragged out of the door and locked away for the rest of her life, and all she knew was he drank tea, had a spouse, and thought her home was too crappy to visit.

"So let's start with three things," she said, urgency burning. "First, I want to know why I was arrested, because I think you know why, whether you issued the order or not. Second, I want to know why you are starving the newts, because—"

"Newts?" Ferala drew back in surprise. "They are forest creatures; they have no role in this."

"Your net. There's a net around this forest, keeping them away."

"They are huge animals; you have not seen them. Sharp teeth and wide mouths. Their talons dig like your pickaxes. Would you have them running with your children? Walking into your homes? In your city, do you not cover windows to keep away the bees?"

Dime hesitated to let on her direct knowledge of the newts, worried about putting them at further risk. So, as she had with the prison guard, Dime diluted her own facts. Except, she reassured herself, what she said was true. "The Ja-lal have information on the newts. That they live on the beaches of the Heartland, cold and starving."

Ferala was staring at the markings on her face with a sad look in his eyes, as if he thought they made her dirty. It solidified her sense that he knew her biology. As if Dime was further gone than he'd realized, referring to herself as a brute and sympathizing with animals. Yes, Dime was reading into it, but his expressions were unmistakable. It was the same pity pyrsi showed her when they learned her father's class. The same pity they'd shown when she said she was leaving the Circles, as if she just wasn't good enough to stay.

"We left them sections of the forest," he said. "But I don't see why you risked coming here just to—"

"You left them sections of the forest without water," Dime rose from the stool. "You're harming them. Much more and you'll be killing them. Is that what you intend for the Ja-lal also? Why won't you answer my questions? What will you do, leader of the Fo-ror, if you cannot stop the flood you describe? Return the Violence? Invite it? Allow it?" Dime's voice was starting to shake but she did not sit back down. "That's what the Ja-lal think you want. Is it? Tell me. Please."

"I will do what I need to do to protect Sha's pyrsi. As I have—" Caught on something, he stopped.

Dime didn't. "I'm not leaving without answers. Chambers is in session, correct? Are they missing you there? Is Seat Neimano asking where you've gone?"

Ferala winced.

"Do you have all turn, High Seat? I only know that I am part of something here, and I'm not leaving until I understand why. And you will not lead me away because I will shout to every pyr in my path *what was done to me*. That it is not the Ja-lal who threaten the Violence. It is *you*. And if it wasn't you, it was someone, and I think you know who. If there is an innocent explanation, I'm waiting to hear it. If the Ja-lal took me from you and this is all their doing, then tell me. Go ahead. But if *you* have done this to me, if *you* have done this to the newts, what else have you done? What else are you doing?"

Well beyond fear or nervousness, fury threw the truth from her lips. "I know that I am biologically Fo-ror. I know that I was born with wings. And I know that you feel you have power over me here, because you have valence and I don't. Well, it's not valence that is dangerous here, High Seat Ferala. It's *me*. And you will *tell* me what is going on."

Ferala sat, stunned, staring into the silence between them. A small rap sounded at the door. He looked frightened for a split stride but then relaxed. "Enter," he said.

Tikinal leaned in, his knot of variegated hair followed by a somber face. He glanced between them before proceeding in with a fresh tray of tea. "I am sorry for the delay, High Seat, but I didn't want to interrupt. Oh. Chambers is in disarray. Seat Neimano is making arguments, but Seat Layanie has refused to start debate regarding the Ja-lal without your attendance."

He hesitated. "I advised them you were taking breakfast. It is unclear whether they will continue or whether a recess will be called. High Guard Ulkanet is waiting for a break in which to speak to Seat Neimano."

As if he'd just commented on the breeze, Tikinal swapped out the tea for one Dime could see steaming from its saucer. He whisked from the room and closed the door again.

Ferala pursed his lips, as if holding back his words. Dime expected another diversionary speech or lecture, but he spoke, now, almost like a normal pyr.

"Near the time of your birth, a disease spread through the Heartland. A blight so terrible it— I cannot describe it. It killed a pyr from inside and out. There was a chance one might recover, but the suffering was so great, it tried the will of our most dedicated healers. Pyrsi referred to it only as the curse."

Dime remembered that Ella had said Fo-ror healed with more difficulty than the Ja-lal, that finding basic remedies for illness was more of a focus for them than the more advanced medical remedies the Ja-lal sought in their enclaves.

"Anger stirred, not just in Pito, but the villages as well. Pyrsi watched their parents, their friends, their lovers, even their children die before them. It was said some cried with uncontrolled relief to learn that it would soon take them also." He started to bring his tea close, then stopped, setting it back down.

"Amongst this anguish, a rumor began that it was contact with the Ja-lal that had caused this curse. That someone had betrayed peace and traveled to the land of the brutes, where they had contracted this foul disease.

"Then the rumor shifted. It was not just that it had spread through contact, but that the Ja-lal had spread this curse on purpose, finally fulfilling their goal of winning the Great War. Of destroying every Fo-ror on Ada-ji and claiming the Heartland as their own, to blast down its trees and stomp over our ashes, swinging their shining blades."

She reeled with new thoughts, sitting back onto the stool to steady herself. She knew that the Violence had been justified in the Great War, but she'd never considered the methods of conducting it. Common things. A blade. An explosive. A *disease*. Associations so damaging that even after the end of War, minds still suffered, considering whether each new tragedy had been inflicted on purpose. Blade size was still regulated in Sol's Reach; she'd never considered why.

"You can imagine what this panic would cause," Ferala continued. "My sources tell me Lodon is in a state of confusion over the mere sighting of our pyrsi there. Imagine if they were dying, first one here, then another, then scores. Paranoia fed the anger, and soon pyrsi were demanding the Seats act, that they rain powers of . . . valence on Lodon, on all the brutes. Destroy them forever so the Violence would never threaten us again."

Dime's hands shook from this story, from the thought of such a disease—and of such fear, inciting pure desperation for the Violence. Her stomach turned. Her mind spun.

She thought of Luja, vis studies. Though Luja had not been born then, the medics of Lodon were skilled; they could have helped. The words burst from her mouth. "The Ja-lal could have helped! Their medics are skilled healers."

"I think we all considered it, in our minds. But the walls we build ourselves are not so easily scaled. No one spoke it. We all looked to the High Seat—it was not I then. She did nothing."

"Not even a quarantine?" Dime couldn't imagine that.

"It was a hyperbole. You are correct; she instituted a state of strict adherence to proclaimed rules. Quarantines, barriers, boundaries.

Animals were swept from villages with tonics, smoke, and noises to keep them away."

"Nets," Dime murmured. Ferala continued to talk, as if releasing something held deeply, as if Dime were not there.

"She did nothing about the Ja-lal. Energized, a group of Seats met in private. I was young then, younger than you. I was Seventh Seat, but the youngest of the Nine. We met within the depths of the caves: Fourth, Sixth, Seventh, and Ninth. We discussed ideas freely and without reserve. Ideas our aged High Seat was unwilling to consider. Some covert. Some rebellious. At first, I roared with the fire of my new power. An ability more powerful than valence: *freedom*."

Ferala clenched his hands together, wringing them. "We traded our ideas, expanded them. First, these ideas tenuously introduced the idea of the Violence. Then, they justified it as the only road to peace. Soon, they openly embraced it. It is not to say that I am so pure as to reject harm in all its forms, but when the Violence is treated as an asset rather than a burden, this is when reason flees and colder hearts prevail." He released his hands.

"My anger had not abated, but neither could I condone our shadow council any longer. The quarantines had shown signs of working. The impact of disregarding our traditions weighed on me. Of disregarding the way of Sha.

"Neimano and I argued, a great fierce argument. He was older than me, but I was from a better family and held a higher Seat. I pled my case; I begged for pause. The Fourth and Sixth Seats sided with me. Our group dissolved, in more ways than one."

Dime knew there was more, and so she waited for Ferala to finish.

"He wanted to make the diamonds sing, he said. Show the Ja-lal our might. Yet, without the Seats' concurrence, he could not mobilize the casters. He would have been imprisoned for treason against Sha. Instead, he returned to one of his older plans, the first that had turned me against him.

Ferala took a deep breath. "There are secrets the High Seat knows that the others do not. I understand, now, why we were wrong to oppose her. We did not know all there was to know.

"Neimano resurrected his rejected plan. He named it Project Diamondsong, evoking the might of our kind. The might we refused to use to defend ourselves, as he saw it. For what could be more powerful than ourselves—using *ourselves* as a weapon. It was . . . for our defense." Ferala closed his eyes, yet Dime did not turn hers away.

"In this plan, ten ba'pyrsi were . . . modified." He opened them again. "They were placed, one by one, over the course of a cycle, in strategic locations, ones near sources of rank and power, believing they would be accepted into Ja-lal society. Neimano knew that the Ja-lal allowed any class to take positions of power. He was so convinced of our superiority, he was sure these small ones would rise to the top.

"Then, when the time was right, they would be informed of their true nature. That they were tendrils of Sha's protection, destined to save their own kind. They would, from their imbedded positions of power—and under Seat Neimano's direction—retake Sol's Reach and restore Fo-ror leadership over the brutes."

Dime spun in a cloud of ideas and horror, without sense of time or danger. There was nothing in this suspended place but she and Ferala, each lost in their own trauma, their gazes finally fully connecting.

"That is horrific," she managed to whisper. As flawed as the Light's Circle was, she could not imagine any of its members doing something so terrible. So cold. Impacting so many lives on just a chance. A shadow of relief flickered that the Circles had not been involved. Had not known.

"It is. I did not know he continued on with it. We were all so relieved to regain some normalcy, and Neimano and I were not then speaking." He leaned back, just slightly.

"The Way of Sha aside, it was a flawed plan, with too much risk.

We told him that. We asked, what if the young grow attached to the Ja-lal? They would not, he insisted. What if their scars were noticed? They would not be, he said. The brutes were self-conscious about irregularities in their skin; they concealed them, injecting them with ink. There must be great differences between us, we insisted. They would notice. He laughed, and said the brutes were unintelligent. They would see what they wanted to."

Dime couldn't excuse the other Seats. Explaining that the plan wouldn't work wasn't the point, though she did sense Ferala knew that. It disgusted her that Neimano could even express such a plan, yet still be allowed to rule. She had seen this in the Circles, with Atti. It was easier for them to look away than to face what they'd enabled. She pushed back these thoughts, not wanting to miss Ferala's story.

"He enlisted an elderly healer, one who was ill and would take the secret with him to Sha. Which he did. I imagine he was threatened or coerced—yet those details rest only with Neimano now."

"Then," Dime asked, wanting to get the whole story before she made sure she never rested eyes on these Seats again, "how did you learn what he'd done?"

"He told us. He told the three of us who had participated. He was too proud of himself not to boast to someone. He had evidence of our involvement: our notes, our handwriting. We had our word to say we had refused him, but that would be tainted by association." Ferala sat up. "If there had been a chance of stopping it, I could have acted. But the deed was done. You see? Speaking out then would have only risked upsetting the tenuous peace we had so thinly regained."

"It could have removed Neimano from power," Dime said. "It could have sent me the truth."

"I am sorry. I have lived with this shame a long time."

"You?" Dime couldn't believe the audacity of the pyr, a pyr who didn't finish his tea if it sat too long. "You have lived with shame? I have lived with this *robbery*. I have lived with a *lie*. I have lived with—"

She wasn't sure how to express the frustration she felt. Her life wasn't a lie. Her life was beautiful. And it wasn't just once that she'd been disrupted. She'd been pulled from a family she never knew, spirited to a strange land. But she'd built a life there. A happy life. Then they'd ripped her out again, denying her the choice to continue her life as it stood. It was their invasion—once and then twice—that infuriated her, whatever the outcome. The outcome was not their business.

Dime loved her life. She loved her family. None of that could or would be taken from her. None of that was diminished. Yet there was a question that must be asked.

"The pyr or pyrsi who would have been my parents." She left it as a fragment, unable to continue.

"There is no record. The ba'pyrsi were the most susceptible to the curse, they comprised many of its deaths. It is my theory that Neimano took ba'pyrsi held in quarantine and declared them dead.

"We have records of many young victims, but to know which were victims of disease and which were victims of Neimano's ploy cannot be discerned. Even Neimano may not know. He is older; his memory does not reach as far with clarity, and he kept no records of lineage."

Dime had gained some small sense of Fo-ror class structure. She knew lineage was important. "When we were to return," she said, "he did not want any bias from our previous class."

Ferala bowed his head.

"And so, we were from lower-class homes. Outer villages. Places where a pyr had no recourse if they suspected."

"It is my theory," Ferala agreed.

"Why now?" Dime heard her own words, a whisper, as if spoken by another.

"The brutes are driven by wealth, Neimano said. He found Ja-lal willing to track certain pyrsi and deliver periodic reports. They were not given details, just instructed on which pyrsi to monitor and where to report. They likely didn't know they were working for the Fo-ror. He hid the true diamonds in his queries, giving many resources to these mercenaries to report on dozens of pyrsi, some important and others not.

"Over the cycles, Neimano began to speak more openly to me of his plans, even now as I am High Seat. He resents my position but keeps me informed. It is a threat, of course. A reminder of what I was party to, of what he knows. It is also an offer, that when he deems it time to act on his plans, it will be my choice whether I stay to lead them."

Dime began to consider what that meant, but dropped the thought at his next words.

"One of the Diamondsong subjects, one of the early ones, surprised him the most. This one he had written off. A dud, as he put it. Placed at the height of the Circles complex, flown to a busy walkway at the height of political season—yet found and taken by a maintenance worker. One who named her, most ironically, Diamond. He laughed at this one, given the grandest of names, yet, the least of the lot.

"Then, despite her unworthy station, she rose through the ranks of the Intel Circle, the organization Neimano had most prized as a source of reenergizing the project—activating it, as he said. As others faltered, Diamond continued to ascend. He kept me eagerly appraised that this pyr, this low-class pyr, might make it to the ranks of the Light's Circle. 'We are almost there,' he gloated."

Dime gasped, the timeline coming into view. "I left. Before I was selected."

"You did," Ferala said, his fingertips pressed together.

"How many of us?" She thought she remembered, but needed to hear it again. To be certain.

"Ten."

Ten. Nine other pyrsi, like me.

"Four have joined memory."

Four . . . dead? That was too many. She was not old, nor would be the others. But, then, five more remained.

"Will you tell me about the others? What you know?" Dime wasn't sure what she'd do with the information, but she was feeling increasingly sure she wouldn't be back here soon. So, whatever she could get.

"Diamond, I urge you, there is more at stake here. Our separation is so tenuous; you must feel it. You do not know the things that I know. What the Great War almost did to our kind. What—"

The firm knock that sounded on the High Seat's door did not wait for an answer.

"High Seat, are you— Oh! Good!" The robed Seat, who Dime now knew to be Neimano, waved his hand over his brow in mock relief. "We were worried in Chambers that you'd fallen ill; Tikinal was nowhere to be found, and, oh!" He stepped back, scowling as if surprised and flustered.

Liar.

"The escaped Ja-lal! You found her. Excellent work, High Seat." He stared at Dime with a focused gaze that Dime avoided. Instead, she sat quietly on the stool, her eyes planted on Ferala's desk, while she tried to think.

If he wanted to gain her cooperation, certainly he'd reveal her biology, her planned role as hero to the Fo-ror. Play the "good agent," even. Why wasn't he?

He began to step toward her, but Ferala regained his composure and raised a hand. "Seat Neimano. I did. Do not approach her; she is skittish. I'm sure you can understand how scared they get."

"*Mmm,*" Neimano said, not moving his gaze from Dime. "Oh, of course. She must be frightened. Always scurrying off, this one."

Dime ran through her options, her heart now thumping in her chest. Though she'd not felt anxiety alone with Ferala, she now felt uneasy. Her sense of danger grew. She glanced between the two leaders—and made a choice.

Standing up, Dime clenched her fists and turned to Neimano. "I demand answers. If he won't provide them, then you will."

Ferala stayed frozen in place.

"First, why was I arrested from my home? You *fairies* have no right to invade Sol's sacred lands, the lands of the Ja-lal. I demand an answer."

"Your name is Diamond?" Neimano asked.

Dime couldn't resist almost spitting out the words, "It is." She remembered Ferala's story. "And you are, Second, no, *Third* Seat?"

Neimano's eyes narrowed, but he gave her a curt nod.

"As I said, I refuse to be denied answers any longer. I want to know why your guards tried to capture me. I want to know why I was put in prison here when I'd committed no crime. Is this Fo-ror honor? To rob one's freedom without cause?"

Neimano stepped forward. "The other. They said you talked to her. Why is she here? Tell me that, first."

It took Dime a moment to understand what he meant. "Agent Rock?" Dime rolled her eyes. "Yeah, I saw her. Low-ranking IC agent; fell from favor a while back. What does she have to do with this?"

Neimano had clearly not predicted the scene he would find here, as he rolled his lips against each other, searching for the best approach. His robes were plainer than Ferala's, but with studded metal trim down the edges. While it was probably supposed to complement his oversize beaded necklace, Dime couldn't help but compare him to a sofa.

Unlike a sofa, his shoulders were unpadded, as Ferala's were as well. She knew it was prejudice on her part, but the drooping natural shoulders provided an odd contrast to the ma'pyrsi's hair and clothes, all of which spoke of their high class and rank.

Neimano's hair was artificially dark, as dark as his naturally aged skin. She didn't yet know whether hair color was simply fashion or had social connotation, but, she realized this elderly pyr was likely in his Eoch. In Sol's Reach, he would have been retired, relaxing at home, revered for his wisdom and knowledge. Even in the Circles, an Eoch would stay on as a consultant only.

As she noted the wide ribbons that laced his dark hair, a thought began to form.

This pyr, it dawned on her, *had my wings removed with a* KNIFE.

As her blood warmed in her fingers and her face, she saw the direction he was staring. Not toward her, but toward her chest. Toward the spot under her tunic where her pendant was hidden. Her diamond. The pieces all fit.

Ferala didn't arrest her, as he'd said. Neimano did, without the other Seats' permission. His guards were working with him. That's why they tried to take her to Neimano, not Ferala. That guard had seen her pendant, in her home. Xe'd told Neimano about it.

Dime didn't understand why her diamond was important, just that it seemed to be. She remembered the High Guard's shock upon seeing it. She remembered Ella's expression, her urging to keep it hidden.

The question was, whether Neimano would reveal its presence in front of Ferala. She bargained not, otherwise he'd have mentioned it already. And why was he calling her a Ja-lal? Not calling her to his side and urging her to assist him?

Watching these two leaders, poised like challenging monarch pieces in a realms game, she knew she couldn't stay here, a pawn in between them. She saw now the mess she had marched into. When Ella said the Fo-ror were honorable, that they eschewed the Violence, Ella had not met Neimano. Dime was not safe. Her family was not safe.

"If you will not answer my questions," she said, "I will take my leave." She hoisted her backpack up over her shoulders. Ferala's eyes flicked from Dime to Neimano and back again. Dime walked toward the door.

"You're going nowhere, *Diamond*," Neimano said with a grunt. "We have more to discuss. And, as you know, you are still under arrest." She looked back; he was still staring at her tunic. His fingers twitched.

"The Ja-lal are not bound by your rules, Seat Neimano." Dime decided to flush it out. Would he tell her, or would he not? That might help her reason through her options later.

"They will be," he growled, and Dime could see his last thread of patience snap. "Walk," he commanded.

At that moment, a familiar rap sounded on the door. An expression flashed across Ferala's face that Dime could not quite read. Fear, or even relief. "Enter," he called. Tikinal slid into the room, carrying a new tray of tea.

"Honorous Seats," he said, "Seat Neimano, my apologies—I wasn't told you were here as well; I should have brought a second tea. Seat Layanie is asking after both of you; I told ver I would find you and report back."

Ferala responded before Neimano could collect his anger. "Clerk Tikinal," he said, his voice raised. "Take our prisoner to the dead caves. Once you arrive, keep her under bars."

"Not the clerk. I will take her myself," Neimano spat. "She escaped once before."

Twice, actually.

Ferala smiled—the same cold, polite smile she'd seen from senior Circles officials a thousand times. "There is no escape possible now that the ruse was discovered. Tikinal, do you promise you will follow my orders?" Ferala walked around his desk and toward Dime, his interlaced braids swaying like pendulums.

"As always, High Seat." Tikinal bowed.

"Then take her to the cages."

"Yes, High Seat."

Ferala stopped and turned toward Neimano. "Seat Neimano, if you would prefer to accompany her, I will go apologize to Seat Layanie for the delay. I can let ver know you have a special interest in the prisoner."

Feeling only danger in this overt discussion of her freedom, Dime almost bolted. Yet she didn't know to what lengths Neimano would go to stop her. And there was something pleading with her in Ferala's eyes. She held her action. Her lips pulled tight.

Ferala leaned in with a few low words for Neimano only. To her side, Tikinal was frantically scribbling something, the notebook angled high toward his chest.

"Come along," Tikinal directed, and Dime, hanging her head

to appear suppressed but more to avoid catching Neimano's eyes, walked with the clerk, aware of every breath, every noise in the room and around her. In slow motion, she recalculated her options with every step. She would not enter that cage again.

Dime followed Tikinal into a corridor, through another tapestry entrance, and out into the more public spaces. "Here," he hissed during a lull in traffic, whisking her with abrupt motions through a door. With a wave of his hand, the door closed and a stone lit above them.

Coughing, Dime saw they were surrounded by brooms and buckets. As Tikinal wriggled into a less awkward position, his wings bumped and rattled against the hanging broomsticks. Trying to imagine what sort of a risk Tikinal was taking, she stayed silent.

He turned his notepad toward her, holding a large engraved pen against it. In a shaky, uneven writing she presumed not to be the writing of the Seats' Clerk, it said:

> My orders:
>
> Do not enter the dead caves. Help her out of the complex through my passage.
>
> Allocate her what supplies she requests.
>
> Make her promise she will go immediately to Sol's Reach, otherwise you will call a guard to assist in her arrest. I trust her word.
>
> - H.S. Ferala

It impressed her that he would sign the note directly. If caught, it would absolve Tikinal, and Dime herself, perhaps, of blame.

The signature was readable, but borderline absurd. Even written with a shaky hand, its flourishes and curvy lines intertwined, almost obscuring the name itself. As she admired it, Tikinal flicked his free hand and the paper ripped out and incinerated. He blew the dust away, giving it a final wave.

Dime found herself nearly nose-to-nose with the clerk. "Sorry if this is awkward," she said, unable to suppress a grin.

"I could have picked a better place, but I figured the Seats don't even know this room exists. I am not accustomed to smuggling alien species past my leaders."

"Your leaders are too uptight," Dime offered.

They both chuckled.

"So, what do you want?" Tikinal's voice shook and she knew, despite his orders, he was now placed in a position of immense risk, one that could have dire consequences. He likely wanted to be done with it, to the extent that he'd incinerated his evidence.

Recalling Neimano's reactions, Dime no longer felt the protection of a world rid of the Violence. She felt fear.

"What do you want?" he repeated.

Dime thought quickly of Rock. She wanted to help her friend get out, but she'd do her no good by getting caught herself. Nor could she compromise the trust of the one Seat who was willing to assist her. This wasn't the right time. Yet— "Tikinal, the Ja-lal prisoner. Will you promise to ensure she's not harmed?" The words stung, but she had seen Neimano's eyes.

Of all that he had taken from her, this was the most.

"Harmed?" Tikinal drank in her implication. "Oh. Yes. I've seen no signs of any escalation to . . . they dislike her more than anything. Yes, I will do what I can." Seeing Dime's expression, he added, "I would never close my eyes to the Violence. Never."

"Thank you," Dime said. She kept trying to think what she needed to get back. She'd lost a climbing hook. Did she have enough food? Balm? What else? She patted her pockets, thinking. Dime almost snorted at her own ridiculous answer, but she'd felt Ador's dice, and remembered. "First, thank you. I am friend to the Fo-ror." Tikinal's unpadded shoulders relaxed a little at those words.

"I'll leave without delay and I promise to travel directly to Sol's Reach. In return, I . . . would accept three gifts." That felt silly to say, but Ella had emphasized that she should refer to needs as gifts.

"First, can I write a note?" Tikinal handed over his notebook and pen and Dime scribbled out a note, struggling to write with the oversized instrument. She folded the paper together. Setting her own backpack down—with a bit more mutual wriggling in the cramped space—she removed a little construction putty and pressed it against the paper, using one of Ador's dice to make an impression.

She handed the sealed note back to Tikinal, along with the notepad. "Please give this, unread, to the Ja-lal prisoner. I promise it won't help her escape or cause harm." Tikinal nodded.

Dime waved the pen, its metal highlights glinting. "May I keep this?" Tikinal shrugged and Dime slid it into her bag.

"Next . . . I'd like a bottle of the best ferm that fairies drink. Not, like, the stuff for a party, not even government stuff. Your highest-class pyrsi—what would they drink on a special occasion? I'd like a good bottle of that, fully sealed. It'll be in my bag while I scale the cliff," she explained.

Tikinal appeared to be biting his lip.

"Last, I have a friend who loves games."

"Games?" Tikinal looked like he was just going to leave.

"Tabletop games; I'm sure you have them here. I want to give him a gift, as he gave me one. Something made by fairies, like a rolling game, or a chips game—" Dime was trying to figure out how to say she wanted something nice without sounding like way too much of a mooch. But, she reasoned, the Seats still owed her a few. "Something really top notch. It can't be too large." She pointed to the bag.

Tikinal actually grinned. "Three, right? That's it?"

Dime grinned back. "Yes, for now."

Tikinal appeared as though he had a thousand things to say and couldn't bring himself to say any of them.

"It's ok," Dime said. "Hey, it was really nice to meet you. I hope you don't get into trouble for this." The thought pinched at her insides. "You can come with me, if you need." She'd meant well by it, but immediately realized the flaws in her offer. It wasn't as if the winged pyr could stroll around Lodon. And without his friends and family.

"My place is here," Tikinal said, his grin disappearing. "I trust High Seat Ferala." Dime nodded, awed by the clerk's bravery. She saw the way Neimano had looked past him, like he was nothing. Maybe that would work in his favor. Maybe Ferala was counting on it.

Dime couldn't worry about that right now. There was too much in her mind, anyway, between Ferala's story and her unanswered questions about Neimano— She still didn't understand this world, and she'd already promised to leave it. The Seats would have to mop their own mess. She glanced away from a big floppy mop.

"I can't risk leaving you here," he said. "We'll get you through Ferala's tunnel first. Neimano shouldn't know about it. *I* shouldn't know about it; I just don't happen to matter. I'll go another way around and meet you."

"If getting the gifts puts you in danger, then we can skip them."

Tikinal actually rolled his eyes at that. "Not returning you to prison might put me in danger. A couple of trinkets from the lounge; *that* I can manage. Besides, the High Seat's orders." Tikinal tilted forward, though not much given their already-close quarters. "He did probably think you'd ask for, you know, socks."

"I have socks." Dime wiggled her toes in her boots. *Harm, I should have asked for boot oil.*

Dime had pushed that far enough.

Tikinal opened the door a bit and peered around the corner. Pausing, he grabbed the large mop. "Hold this," he said. "Just in case."

Dime lifted the mop and Tikinal pushed the floppy strands over her head. "Consider it our best invisibility cloak," he joked. "*Tale of the Traveler?*" he asked, seeing Dime's blank expression. "No?"

"We have cloak issues up my way, sorry."

Together they walked out, Tikinal chattering a stream of nonsense while pointing to various corners, appearing to instruct her on how to clean the passages. Not a single pyr even glanced their direction.

In a passageway that must have been near the kitchen, for Dime could hear splashing water and clanking pots, Tikinal waved an arm, and a portion of the wall pushed back into itself, leaving an opening.

"No time for goodbyes. Now that's our best mop," he said, taking it back from her. "When you get outside, hide, and wait. If I'm not there to meet you in . . . two spans, then leave." Not waiting for a response, he ushered her into the opening. Before she could say anything to the pyr, the wall had closed again and she was alone in a very pitch dark, completely silent place.

The fairies probably waved on the lights. "My life," Dime murmured, using her hands to feel her way along a winding passage.

Her sense of time had been warped without the reminder of bells, yet it didn't seem like more than two takes had gone by when the passage ended. Not feeling a door handle, she hoped the door didn't require valence too. Tikinal probably hadn't considered that, so she hoped this was the push side. With both hands, she gave it a hearty heave, and squinted at the bright light of Sol glaring in over the top of a tall hedge.

Trying to ignore the overwhelming smell of rot, she pushed the heavy door shut behind her, grunting as it finally clanged back into place. Running her hand along the textured wall, she marveled at how seamlessly the door blended in.

As the door had no handle on this side, she could not have found it again, let alone opened it. He did say to wait outside, right? She covered her nose, glancing with regret at the now unopenable panel.

Still, she took a moment to note the surroundings. Finding a stone with an unusual shape, she twisted it into the soil to mark the spot, just in case.

Tikinal had said to hide, but was staying behind the hedge hiding? She wasn't sure. The area smelled so *bad*. Creeping along its edge, she peered through a thinner section. As she'd suspected, this appeared to be a compost area for the complex. Piles of old food and wrappers spread over a field, through which scruffy little trees had started to poke through.

She wasn't going to go hide in that either.

Keeping a sleeve over her nose, she tried not to worry about the passing of the takes as she leaned back and waited. She replayed

Ferala's words in her mind, and Neimano's as well, remembering the details so she wouldn't forget them, trying to find any additional clues she had missed.

The thought of the remaining five victims weighed on her, just as much as the four who had died did. Why had they died? Did any of the living know their biology? Would they admit it? Without clues, would she just walk through Lodon asking to see pyrsi's bare backs? To feel their tattoos for any telltale bumps?

If they knew, it wasn't her job to expose them, but if they didn't know, wouldn't it be her obligation to tell them? She wasn't sure.

She'd been happy in Sol's Reach; maybe they were too. Was disrupting them now, in a place they'd lived their lives, an even greater cruelty? Or did pyrsi always deserve their truth? Ferala had asked about Sol's Reach. He'd grown agitated when Dime asked about the others. Perhaps he'd considered those same questions. And then Neimano had strolled in, calling her Ja-lal like it was an insult.

She didn't understand either of these pyrsi. Ferala's inaction felt inexcusable at first sweep, but could his taking action have caused more harm? Had he consciously decided to leave the victims uninformed? Could confronting Neimano have resulted in a coup, with Neimano openly in charge instead of precariously in check?

And Neimano, he made less sense—though, she realized, it wasn't his desire to overtake the Ja-lal that confused her. If he truly believed the Ja-lal threatened harm to the Fo-ror, if he truly believed they were lesser, then his desire to control them could be explained. Even his lack of aversion to the Violence—she found it abhorrent—but she could link it to the same lack of empathy she'd seen in Lodon. Belief in absolutes lent itself to such logic.

Ella was right. The Great War had never been resolved; it had only been pushed into stasis, fostering such logic as Neimano's.

What confused her was why he hadn't tried, then, to recruit her. The whole point of his plan, she now understood, was to leverage her influence for the good of the Fo-ror: influence she still had, in her contacts, her insight, even her appearance. He was now willing to toss that aside?

The act couldn't have been for Ferala's benefit; Neimano knew that Ferala knew the truth. Then, after her own bit of redirection, he'd not wanted Dime to know. Which didn't fit his plan. Unless something had changed. But what?

In some sense, she regretted leaving the complex so soon, and considered going back, as Rock had, and letting herself be imprisoned again, if only for more answers.

No.

She wasn't going in that cage again, nor would she endanger her ability to return for Rock. And she needed to get back to the city, back to her family. They weren't safe; she understood that now.

She jumped at a rustling in the hedge. "Are you back there?" She recognized Tikinal's voice.

"Yes, here." She shook one of the branches.

"Come over this way!" She could just make out a gesture leading down the wall. He wasn't flying; it made sense he wouldn't want to draw attention to this spot. Dime pulled up her bag and jogged down the side of the wall until she found a space to squeeze through. "Ow!" she said, glaring at the branches scratching her hands.

"We fly over it," he said, with a sigh. "Sorry, I didn't consider that. Now, over here, away from that stench." They walked together over a hill, into what seemed to be a storage yard for fallen trees. Piles of lumber rested under a wooden roof. The smell here was of fresh air and cut wood, and Dime breathed with relief.

"I can't believe you sat by the compost," he said, his wings flapping a little. "That's why I said to hide!"

"I didn't want to confuse you."

"But you have, anyway. How did you endure the smell?"

Dime decided not to tell him about the bells she'd recently spent covered in sewage.

He handed her a largish package, wrapped in paper and tied securely with cloth handles. "Get away before you unpack this. Just take it for now. You need to go." He chuckled. "And the next story I read about a pyr who's granted three wishes, I'll hope it's not a pen, a drink, and a game. I am questioning your survival skills." He hesitated at the end of the sentence, as if unsure what to call her.

"I'm not sure we've formally met," Dime said, surprised to realize it. "I am Fe'Dime. I used to work for the Circles—our government—then I quit."

"Ma'Tikinal," he returned with a nod. "I work for the Seats and will enjoy thoughts of this unachievable quitting fantasy over a ferm in the near future."

"No, don't. I'm the one making the bad choices."

"If you mean waiting for me behind the compost heap, I agree. Otherwise, this has been my pleasure. Now, listen. There is a stairway on the far edge of the city. It's old and heavily damaged, but should help you return to the top."

"It's ok," she said. "I've got climbing equipment." She'd lost the one hook, and had left several spikes lodged where she'd last climbed down, but she should be fine.

"I've not climbed it myself, so I don't know how passable it is; I just thought maybe it could help you." He handed her a tri-folded paper, neatly sealed with wax. "Here, this is what I know of the location."

Dime had considered asking Tikinal a few more questions. About Neimano and Ferala, what he knew of any plans. Yet, here, with the pyr putting himself at risk to help her—for he hadn't been under orders the first time he'd done it in front of Neimano's study—and with the feeling of goodwill between them, she couldn't ask him to take one step further. She wouldn't.

Instead, she smiled. "I don't know why the Heartland needs the Seats when they have you." She realized the words sounded condescending as she said them; she hadn't meant it that way and tried to recover. "I just mean that I've worked around leaders a long time. In Lodon." She pointed the way Tikinal had just indicated. "You strike me as someone I would follow."

Tikinal looked more uncomfortable at her second statement than he had at her first. "The Ja-lal, you must have such interesting perspectives. Here, I have the lot that I have. That Sha gave me, as they say. I am a clerk, my parents were clerks, and theirs before them. And I made it here, of all places, so what better could I have done? It's not something you consider in any other light."

A substantial silence followed, during which Dime was certain he was thinking about how much better he'd be than some of the Seats. She raised an eyebrow, and Tikinal sighed. "They couldn't lace their tree shoes without me."

"Maybe someturn they'll realize that. Actually, they won't. But, for what it's worth, I know it. From afar, anyway."

The smile they exchanged reminded Dime of home. Not to say, her specific home, but that time, not so long ago, before everyone was a stranger, and every step uncertain. He reminded her of old friends, of Circlemates, of those cycles when the bells had passed by in a comfortable rhythm.

She'd tipped that cart herself, it was true, but if she'd known how much of a change it would be— No, she'd still have done it. Yet a fondness returned at remembering how nice it was to have friends and see familiar faces. Maybe, someturn, she'd see Tikinal again.

"Thank you for everything. Please thank the High Seat as well."

Tikinal's mouth twitched. "I will."

She watched with a bit of awe as Tikinal flew off. Balancing the cloth handles of the bundle in her fingers, she pried open the note paper to see what Tikinal had sketched out for her. From his traced drawings, she could see that she was already nor of the city, essentially against the Great Cliff. If she hugged the cliff's base, she should be able to follow it along until she found the staircase, or perhaps its remnants.

Chiseled stone would be her clue, he'd written. So Dime, as she walked, kept an eye out for any stone that was cut, not natural. Just as she began to worry she'd missed it, a jagged edge almost tripped her. Searching around, she found other pieces, parts of an old pathway.

Rummaging through her backpack, she took out a set of claws and other climbing supplies, replacing them with the cloth-bound package. She thought about resting, but she'd promised to leave as soon as she could.

She trusted Tikinal would deliver the note to Rock, and Rock would understand why she'd had to leave for now. Just in case the note fell into the wrong hands, she'd been somewhat cryptic, but she'd written in terms she knew Rock would understand. Realizing Rock had given away her own escape to help Dime had tugged at her mind, but she'd promise to return to the Heartland, and her next priority had to be ensuring her family's safety. The best she could do, for now, was to promise Rock she would not be forgotten.

And she wouldn't be.

Her backpack secured into place, she wrapped her hands, checked the straps, and took large steps up the rocks, until she reached the rock face and the climb truly began.

"Staircase" was a generous term for the passage. It was more like a common climbing spot for travelers, who had chiseled large ledges into the rock to allow for rest. These had been created over what looked like many cycles, with some heavily crumbled or buried under thick scruff.

No matter their state, the results were still appreciated, for she hadn't gone up the cliff before, and the climb was long, hard work. The ledges were a welcome break from the concentration, and definitely to her aching muscles.

Reaching a larger ledge, she finally stopped for a meal, though she wasn't going to risk a fire. She unwrapped her dusty, sore hands, and spared a little of her water to rinse them off.

Rummaging in her backpack, she grimaced at what remained of Wayniam's root chips; they must have been cooked with oil that had leaked through the paper wrapping. Fortunately, the greasy bundle had wedged in between her spoon and cooking pan; she didn't want to be the one to tell Ella she'd stained her nice new clothes with food she'd stashed from prison.

She took all her critiques back once she popped the first cold, greasy chip in her mouth. It was delicious, satisfying, and worthy of the view in front of her.

Here, nestled against the side of the Great Cliff, she could see over the treetops of the forest—a sea of green bumps as vast as the plains of her home, spreading as far as she could see in either direction.

In the distance, she saw what must be Pito, identifiable by the thin columns of smoke snaking up from the treetops, and also from the occasional structure that poked through.

Dime was too far away to see anything specific, but had the idea of a high-class family, dining on a treetop deck. Maybe one of them was peering at the cliff through a telescoping glass. Just in case, Dime waved.

The few fairies she'd met seemed less enamored with the trees than she'd expected. The trees and their elevated views were to them a normal backdrop for their lovingly decorated homes. Dime knew she could never have that perspective. Spending as much time as she had in the center rooms of the towers gave her a passionate appreciation for windows, one she knew she'd never lose.

And the trees . . . these stunning trees. Grand trees, not the carefully planted ornaments of Lodon. How could anyone live amongst them and not revere every moment? Dime allowed herself one more take to soak it all in, and then, repacking her bag, she proceeded back up the cliff.

Her arms ached, but she believed she was almost to the top. She couldn't see exactly because of the bright glare of Sol against the cliff's face above her. Tiring of the long climb, she pulled herself on, planting a few new spikes where she didn't trust the ledges, and forcing herself to focus on each tie and pull of the ropes, each stretch to a new ledge.

With each pull upward, Dime thought again about her steps. She replayed Ferala's words in her mind. Her energy had been focused on learning the truth. She'd done so to an extent. But now what should she do? What was next?

Her plan before all of this had been to start a music school. She supposed she could do that still, but where? In Lodon? Where Sol's Pillars might start a revolution at the sight of her return?

She could probably twist a story about being taken and then released, but even if she could bring herself to do so, who would believe it? Every pyr now knew she'd been taken by fairies, and there had to be a reason why. They'd demand to know it. Nor would this keep her safe from Neimano, should he decide again that she was his to capture.

Or, she supposed, she could tell the truth. She was a victim of the fairies, not a conspirator. And she'd like to stay in Lodon and live out her life. Would the Circles run her out? Would they allow her to stay, as Suzanne had, secluded on a remote edge? Would they drive her away? What about Sol's Pillars; her very presence would upset every form of leverage they had over their followers.

Dime's children loved Lodon. They would not want to be sent away, into hiding, when they'd done nothing wrong. Yet she couldn't see how they could continue to thrive among neighbors who marked them as associating with monsters. Even now, they weren't safe. She remembered Neimano's cold stare, and forced herself to accept this.

There was no going back; of this Dime now felt certain. Contact was on the verge of cascading between Ja-lal and Fo-ror, and then no one would be safe from Neimano, and Sol's Pillars, and whoever else was out there eager for tensions to spark.

Ferala had asked her if she wanted peace. Of course she wanted peace, but at what cost? At what risk that instead of peace, she would restart a War?

One way or another, change was happening. Maybe Dime needed to help guide that change. She couldn't rely that someone else would.

But—why her? Why did she have to be the one? Why hadn't anyone else stepped out to lead the charge? No, the Free Winds had. Others had. But they were kept muted, kept in check by a government designed to serve them. Controlled by the fear of what breaking out could cause.

Dime wasn't sure she could do what the Free Winds couldn't.

She longed to talk to Dayn. Dayn, he'd help her talk through it. The idea of returning to someone she could fully trust, someone she could tell every bit of this to without any thought of motive, comforted her more than she could allow herself to consider right now.

And, so as she reached the top of the cliff and Sol's Reach again stretched before her tired eyes, Dime set aside the actions that were not yet clear, and moved to the front of her mind the one that was. She would find her family and ensure they were safe. After that, she'd have decisions to make.

Dime didn't choose this path, but the idea that she could do something with it lingered in her mind. She'd quit her career, but she hadn't quit herself. She hadn't lost her skills, her life lessons, her friends. A pyr who had done her best all these cycles, she didn't have to be in one particular place to make a difference.

And that's where Neimano had it wrong. Proximity to power made an easier path to influence, but the pyr xemself was the source of xyr own power. And he could put Dime right back in that alley, and she'd climb out of it again. And again. Not until she reached the top, but until she reached where she wanted to be.

Right now, Dime wanted to be back with her family.

And that's where she was going to go.

Eɴᴅ ᴏꜰ Pᴀʀᴛ 02

ABOUT THE AUTHOR

E.D.E. Bell was born in the year of the fire dragon during a Cleveland blizzard. With an MSE in Electrical Engineering from the University of Michigan, three wonderful children, and nearly two decades in Northern Virginia and Southwest Ohio developing technical intelligence strategy, she now applies her magic to the creation of genre-bending fantasy fiction in Ferndale, Michigan, where she is proud to be part of the Detroit arts community. A passionate vegan and enthusiastic denier of gender rules, she feels strongly about issues related to human equality and animal compassion. She revels in garlic. She loves cats and trees. You can follow her adventures at edebell.com.

Continue Dime's story in . . .

Part 03: Heart

edebell.com/diamondsong